Stanky Banky

By
Tre Prince

Cadmus Publishing
www.cadmuspublishing.com

In the city of South Central Los Angeles, ain't nothing sweet – but it's cake. Where low riding, riding Harley's to driving luxury, sport, and foreign cars; rocking designer brand everything; living and partying in plush fabulous condos, houses, and mansions in the hills, is all for style and play.

But to play in these streets you have to have your weight up, be connected, and know your way to the bag. So bank robbing, jacking, scheming, pimping, prostitution, networking, flopping, drug dealing, to working a 9 to 5 or opening a business et cetera is all a means to financial gain. As a hustle, game or trade. But don't sleep; South Central Los Angeles isn't just fun and play. It is too an epic center of profound intellect thinkers and political revolutionaries. From where great leaders, once greater followers, rise up to set the tone or to carry the torch in the city and throughout the nation. Where structure is protocol, and discipline is embraced. But too, the land of gangbanging and head busting; and no matter who or what you are: from a sucka to a busta, Y.G. to an O.G., a square-playa or gangsta, Crip or Blood; man or woman, black or brown, everyone knows their place and falls in line. Those who don't, or buck, or somehow forgets, are quickly reminded. Even those who only come to town to visit.

Stanky Banky

CONTENTS

Introduction 1

Studio 83 6

The Liqk.. 12

Heart & Hustle.. 15

83rd Street Apartments 22

Chipmunk 27

Tiny Trey Soljah... 30

Roscoes'.. 34

Steady Scheming ~ THA Playboy Killa 37

Crush Groove: Private and Industrial Security Inc. 41

Orange'mist. 44

Las Vegas 48

Headquarters 54

House of Blues 58

Ain't Shit Sweet. 62

The Full Moon. 72

Divine Trio 80

The Sit Down.. 87

INTRODUCTION

Inside this spacious, interior designed, high-end furnished, upscale executive office suite, sits a large prestigious man upright in an expensive lush leather chair behind a just as expensive large Oakwood desk. The name title stationed above the desk reads: C.E.O and the immaculate cinnamon color suit and tie worn accommodates the certifications. A rich earthly aroma fills the suites central air from the large plants stationed about, intertwine with fresh leather and wood to largely concoct the smell of success. Once upon a time though, this now living legend was once a multi-millionaire hoodlum that later fell from riches and succumb to drug addiction, homelessness, and incarceration, before bouncing back and rising to grace.

The prestigious C.E.O., who's now more powerful than ever, interlocks his fingers and rest his hands upon the Oakwood. His eyes lay attentively on the two younger men before him, his prestigious protégés, seated in lush comfort chairs opposite his desk.

The two were once gangbanging rascals until he showed them a better way.

"So what brings the two of you here today? I'm quite sure that the reason is cultivating. There has been a lot of growth between us all over the years past, in which I humbly admire. So go ahead and water me with your thoughts; enlighten me."

Executives in their own right, the two prestigious protégés sit before their mentor, for now over a decade, and together they hold a meeting of the minds.

"To get straight to the point of why we're here big homey," begins one of the two young adults both now in their late 20's, and dressed in suits of their own. He speaks with youthful wisdom and ambition, "Me and the lok is going to need the keys to the city. But not on some celebrity binge, where we' getting into clubs and bars for free. That'll come on its own with our presence being announced. Instead, we need'um how when Suge Knight ran Death Row records and the D.A. office or one-time wouldn't charge or fuck with him-"

"Yeah," interjects the second of the two prestigious protégés in a deep tone, his voice maturing with patience over the years. He speaks with clarity. A glance taken apologizes for not meaning to cut off his right hand groove-dog. "Because since we've all been back in L.A. now as our primary residence, me and the homey been in and out the streets abroad more frequently. To that point, we see a lot that has changed and still changing. There's different but potentially better pieces, though without proper fitting, to the puzzle we see. Then next, the Groove Line is looking strong again like how once was the Hoova Connect back in the day." An historical era of their gang's history between the late 80's and early 90's when power, wealth, and respect was all one order.

"However, without a different direction taken it will shortly end as did the era before, and never reach its greater potential," again the voice of youthful wisdom. "Not only that, but overall, the streets of L.A. in general will never be what it can be as a whole if somebody don't step up and seize the opportunity that's out here in bringing it together. Our vision is to be the movement that does and that makes sense out of this street shit. While at the same time stump and leave our foot print in the industry." His eyes lock with his mentor's. The ambition is clear.

"This is where the keys come into play. There is going to be, I'm sure, some blue collars behind desks in their offices, how you are here, who're not going to like the change that's coming but have keys of their own. However, even Bobby Fisher was known to respect a great move or check mate. And so will the next man or woman. Especially when our push becomes too strong to challenge or stop!" The one with the deeper voice leans forward, "This is where the keys come into play."

The two prestigious protégés now sit back into their seats and take to silence. They each can see the wheels turning within the mind of their mentor and O.G. who has the respect, title, and power both in the streets and in corporate America abroad, to push buttons or open and close doors at will. But the nature of such a request before this calculative man with power has to be considered thoughtfully. Much could be at risk in being destroyed, after all that's been built, if the era when Suge Knight ran Death Row records is repeated. Already the West Coast, as far as in the entertainment business goes, hasn't been the same since. A lot of stone walls are still up and can't be budged since after the deaths of 2pac Shakur and Biggie Smalls. And then there is still the L.A.P.D Rampart division scandal. So this isn't a quick nor easy decision to make; not even for a wise teacher that trusts his pupils.

"Look," begins the protégé who is of patience and clarity, seeing that their request isn't a light one. "We're out here now big homey and feel obligated to do something other than just speaking on it like too many are already doing. You yourself taught us that a man can't receive favorable results from sitting around and just talking. It eventually becomes whining and gossip," the eyes meet. The moral principle reciprocated is greatly acknowledged. "With what we're asking of you, will help change a lot of the goofy shit going on out here in L.A.; and on the West Coast period: All the homo and lesbo shit that then got out of hand amongst our kind, in it being an accepted norm; that's not a part of the original man's culture. Then too, all this experimenting with all different types of drugs, mimicking the dress, drama, and fake shit most of these reality shows got people on like it's cool and fly but really got us looking stupid as fuck. None of it is L.A.'s identity. It might be what their on in the south or back east somewhere; that's them. We have our own flaws without having to adopt or be influenced by anyone else's. On the set!"

"Not just that," now joins the second of the two with youthful wisdom, "But we can also dead a lot of this gangbanging and killing in the city; our biggest flaw. By restructuring the minds of the streets to thinking and doing things from a proper train of thought. Like in how you did with me and the lok, and then we both later done within our own circle that's all eating and shitting good." A fact of the two's legally legit million dollar crew.

The silence now returns. But only momentarily. The unlocking of the mentor's hands gives the silent cue that all that has been said is understood. Now the floor is his.

He leans back into his adjustable chair and closes his eye briefly. Wisely pondering his next words before speaking. Ready, his eyes open back and fall again, attentively, on his two soldiers. With a deep voice and the spirit of a guerilla, he grabs hold of their spirits' attention.

"There's no key greater than the key to unlock doors, seen or unseen. However, the hand that turns the key must be disciplined in knowing the power of the key it possesses," his eyes lock. He speaks in an even tone. "In you two my fellow comrades, I believe in and trust without doubt. You overwhelm me gracefully with your growing spirits. Then also, your grooves are impeccable. Nevertheless, know that what you are requesting affords no room for error. Not one! Therefore, cover your tracks at all times and at any cost; leave no threat around that can come back to harm you, us, or anything that we stand for. And always take care of home court first and foremost. Meaning: strengthen the core of your body, team, for in case it ever loses its head, that pertains to the either of you or both ever falling, then the body doesn't fall with you but instead grows another head. A true wise successor puts insurance on his legacy. That way nothing you've put it all on the line for will be in vain," the two protégés can see the irony of truth in the mentor's wisdom. For he has secured his own legacy through their legacy to be. "Furthermore, use sound discretion before every move made. And never act off of impulse. But most importantly, believe and trust in the Creator to ultimately guide and protect you along the way. This is Spiritual Law. Therefore, the each of you must develop your own individual higher self. Because you are the Spirit of God that you trust and believe in. HE made you in HIS image. Which makes you ONE. Last, but not least; Groove In Silence! Make it the code of the streets! Am I understood Chipmunk, and Tiny Trey Soljah?"

In chorus, "Overstood! Guerilla Joe."

STUDIO 83

I'm in a 2-year lease Maybach/ but don't question that/ b'cuz my enns peel back/ like Quran pages./ It's like, what I need with Louis V loafers/ when on my next night out – Im rock'n Mauri Gators/ give me pens in the kite mag for spiting tuberculosis/ and spreading ill bars amongst the masses/ Quarantine me dog/ I'm about to fuck off/ leave my sperm bank DNA for generations'...

Inside of the recording sound booth a lyricist spits bar after bars over a smooth banging track. His body sways from side to side shirtless, inked with tattoos, and sporting a thick gold rope chain shining with a nice medallion. Around his wrist drips a Tag Hever Monaco watch; a $6000 piece on the low. Made for classmen of taste than for show and boast. The lyricist is a gentleman of class and style.

Along inside Studio 83, a small crowd hangs about in a designated lounge area. Aside from the recording session, a social networking atmosphere is live and vibing. However, the slick groovy rhymes flowing from the booth through surround speakers is the primary focus of attention for most in attendance. Even after the incog walks into the place looking incognito: baseball cap pull down low over the brow and wearing a coat with its collars flipped up…

'The Male Rose on Melrose/ sipping umbrella drinks/ and brunching with accountants on my Wall Street/ I give a shout out to me/ still breath'n no life support/ misquote- b'cuz my hustla been a life support/ got me living in quarters with 20ft ceilings/ on acres of private property/ Im balling homey/ And Im dating- no promises with corporate cougars/ the types that fly me out and all expensives paid'…

The incog heads straight over to the man in charge. Anyone taking notice can see that there's a music air about the fellow. He's at least familiar with his surroundings.

"Hey, TS; how's it been brother? And who's that in the booth rhyming over this dope track? The bars are catchy, and he has a nice delivery. I like his sound," compliments the incog.

TS, a dark skin, medium athletic build brotha, standing five foot eight and rocking a short fade fresh haircut, is also known as Tiny Trey Soljah. He turns from the music boards and engineer to greet his awaited guest's arrival.

"Oh, what it do, Ron. Yeah, that's 'da intellectual lok Tre Hakim a.k.a. Male'Rose, on his corporate gangbanging shit. He smooth. In fact, he's a part of the label now. We're recording his first album. I'll need you to do his photoshoot. But for now, what's up wit' it?" Tiny Trey Soljah says to the incog. Whose name is Ron. Ron, a tall lean Middle-Eastern Turkish, in his mid-thirties, doesn't respond right away. Suddenly he's absorbed with looking around the studio and taking it all in for the first time. And is impressed.

The lounge area of this spacious recording studio holds a full bar with stools, covering a section of about one hundred and fifty-nine square feet of marble tile flooring. The other thousand square feet of the lounge is soft carpeted. Several men and women all loath about on lush couches and sofa seats indulging in music writing, puffing loud, sharing laughs and conversations, along with drinks. A 72" smart TV fills a good portion of the wall it occupies, depicting multiple screens illustrating from: sports games, a movie, and UTube music videos; to porn, and Instagram pages. Two young adult women, one chunky, the other slim petit, but both sexy and gorgeous as fuck, goof around on a PS4 game system plugged in also on the t.v.

Ron finally returns his attention, but still approving of the atmosphere about him. Large frame photos of great musicians: Bob Marley, 2Pag Shakur, Biggie, Marvin Gaye, Sade, B.B. King, Phil Colins; both living or passed on, all hang about the walls of the place.

"Oh, my bad there for a second; I heard you TS. But yeah, I stopped by to finally check you out since you've opened up here. I like this spot. It's nicely arranged. And it has a feel of comfort, purpose, and objective. It's fitting; I like it. Makes me want to bust a rhyme, make a beat, or write a melody," humors Ron.

Tiny Trey Soljah gives a small smile then looks around at his establishment as if noticing it for the first time.

"It's straight. Would you like a drink or anything?"

Ron denies the offer, making it clear that he's there for something that's strictly confidential.

"I came to run something by you," enlightens Ron while giving a knowing look.

"A'ight speak on it. You have that situation lined up for me?"

"Yep. It's all secure. The greatest time to catch her with her panties down is this weekend while she's performing at the VMA's," secretly advises Ron of the intel he's been putting together for over two months now.

Tiny Trey Soljah walks over to the bar, followed by Ron. He orders a bottle water, pays for it, and quenches his thirst. He realizes then that he hasn't drank any liquids in over two hours and after smoking some good cotton mouth weed. Not truly his thing to do, in smoking weed, though every now and then he indulges.

Now feeling refreshed, Tiny Trey Soljah returns his full attention. He first met Ron a couple years back, back when he started his private and industrial security company called, Crush Groove, managed by his uncle alongside him. Ron, a freelance photographer, did a photo prop for the company later used for marketing and advertisement purposes. Aside from his work with him, Ron had published work in several magazine titles such as: US Weekly, People, and Red Bulletin. Ron's craft gave him the intel in knowing the locations and layouts of many famous celebrity homes. Which is why he's here to see him.

"And you sure she's holding thick in there?" Asks Tiny Trey Soljah.

"Hey bro, this is her main house in California; trust me. Plus, it's the VMA's weekend. Everybody that's somebody, and are coming out, is looking to do it big. So they're bringing out their best. You know, just to flaunt. Rich white people like doing so too; if not more than others. Especially the younger ones. And especially one that's selling millions of records and gets paid a quarter million to do a show. Besides, most have insurance on anything they own of value. And that makes many of them careless at times."

Rubbing his nose now for a sixth consecutive time, Ron looks at Tiny Trey Soljah who pays it no mind. It is already understood that he's a coke head. Just as well that he doesn't make very much money snapping pictures. Not as he would like to anyway. But with the business at hand, he is looking to strike for ten grand. And maybe double that if his info provided scores a hefty net.

Tiny Trey Soljah soaks in the intel and receives the torn piece of paper with additional information needed, that Ron hands to him, to complete the mission. He'll later pass it along to a crew of his homeboys from his neighborhood that are into flopping houses as a profession. Which obviously isn't his lane of business. However, his part taken in this future job is a part of a calculated chess move in play. And for good reason.

For one, matha fuckas aren't going to keep partying in L.A., bringing and leaving their filth and dirty morals behind without paying tax to the souls of these streets. So in that regard, he feels no sympathy and instead sees this liqk as a way for putting something into his homies pockets; in helping feed those. Which is an obligation he feels loyal to with honor. And so, he will not be asking nor looking for a share of the future take. That would be the least in reward from the scheme. Instead, his mind is trained on a reward far more greater than a house burglary heist. He wanted domination...

Five minutes later Ron leaves the studio headed on his way to cop a much needed bag of blow. He's feeling excited about the score from the information he just provided. But at the same time he's, too, a bit jittery. He pray and hopes that nothing falls back on him in biting him in the ass later. Only after first considering a few other candidates to shop the info to did he later decide to go ahead with Tiny Trey Soljah, and who willingly just coughed up five grand up front. That certainly made him the more lucrative candidate. The others were going to be upset but business was business. And money seals all the deals in this business...

Tiny Trey Soljah returns back to the music boards and his seat beside the engineer. Out from the recording booth appears Male'Rose, the rich corporate Play Boy Killa. His swag is definitely in a lane of its own. Tiny Trey Soljah calls him over to have a quick word.

"Say, Hoova boy, you sound groovy on that track," compliments Tiny Trey Soljah.

"That's what's up, hoove. I have some catchier slap though. Schoolboy Q is pulling up in a minute. Wait till you hear this corporate gangbanging shit I did with groove and Traffic." Boast Male'Rose with confidence as he puts on a leather sleeveless Versace vest. He stands at 6'4 in a pair of patent leather and suede Versace boots.

"Bet. I can't wait to hear that. In fact, let me spin off real quick. I'll be right back."

Tiny Trey Soljah spins off to his office to make a private phone call. He has to get the ball rolling with the info Ron has given him. This coming weekend is the Viewer's Choice Music Awards. And he now had the hottest diva, currently in pop music, lined up to book for her safe of cash and jewels. A valued estimate of around 2.3 million in total. Or more. The take is surely to make world entertainment news. Which is a big part of the plan.

But in the streets, every flopper and robber around L.A. not in the liqk are definitely going to be in their bodies about missing it. Now the bar is going to be raised for every go-getter to strap up their boots in a bag hunt for the next big sting after a liqk so sweet. Putting more celebrities and every financial institute with that bag, at high risk. And fuck waiting around for the summer to then strike something to shine. All seasons of the year were made to shine in, in L.A.

THE LIQK

Slurp. Slurp…umm. Slurp.

"Awh, fuck. Like that. That's how you feel?"

Slurp. Umm. Slurp. Hmm.

The thug lays back into a musty couch he sits on, enjoying his knob being slobbed on by a thick, chocolate, sundae shake he spotted just merely an hour ago footing it to nowhere in particular. Quickly he had pulled alongside her inside of his Dodge Durango truck, on 26's, smoking a blunt of Moon Rock. And out of all the things, it was the weed that ultimately helped entice this weed berry. Her dark lips, and open toe sponge slippers, were a dead giveaway to the thug's instant stereotype of her. Even with her feet and nails being done, and the fact that she wasn't busted, she was still a THOT. Also a nympho, that once high on some good weed loved to suck dick.

Over on the wall before the couch, a flat screen television plays music videos. The volume is down low but high enough to still hear the program playing. The thug peers up at the throw-back 'Tip Drill' video through sleet eyes while enjoying his com-panion's freaky fetish. Then suddenly his eyes widen all the way; and fast. On the TV the program has been interrupted by ce-lebrity breaking news. A MTV news reporter, reports: "Over this weekend's events, during the VMA's, major pop star singer, Britney Spears, small mansion home in Malibu, California was broken into. A whopping total of $4 million in cash and jewelry was stolen. We'll have more on this story as it develops. But don't worry, no one was hurt. The singer nor anyone else were present during the break in."

The thug, who too is heavy in the streets and known for chas-ing a bag, goes limp after speeding up the strong release that nearly gives him brain freeze. All that now crosses his mind is 'the Liqk.' Oblivious to the breaking news, the nympho carries on with sucking after swallowing a cum fill and believes that her talents is the cause for the body language she is now receiving from the mentally drained thug, before finally spitting a limp dick out from her mouth.

"Did you like that. I told you that I was a beast!"

"Fuuuck. This shit crazy, cuzzz," groans the thug, feeling sick. A small spell of envy could be detected in his tone.

Right at the moment the thug can care less about what this rip-per slipper pounded her chest about having a mouth that spoke volumes without words uttered, and as he hurry and dresses his mind is zoned in on the sweet liqk he let slip out of his hands. He quickly reaches for his phone.

Stanky Banky

"Yeah, I heard. In fact, I too just peeped it on MTV a second ago. Somebody hit the liqk before we did. But I know one thing, the boy bet not had put anybody else on the liqk. His ass owe big time if he did that!" the receiver on the call swears.

"Definitely, if he did," growls the thug still in his body. "But at the same time, for real- for real, fool a coke head. He likely had shopped the liqk around to ten different matha fuckas. So, really, it's on to the next big sting. Though if we catch his ass some- where, he will be taxed! Anyways, is matha fuckas still politicking over giving Shaq back his Superman chain?"

"Shit, from my understanding he got it back already. He coughed up some bread for it tho'. Ain't nothing sweet. Oh, but trip. The main person who was politicking for it back, turns out he's an informant; working with the people. That shit in the newspaper and all. And he was tied in with the Nation."

"Oh, yeahhh. Well one thing about it, the Nation don't harbor no rats. So his ass bet not get caught in the trap. But listen, fuck all that. We need to get on to the next liqk. Shit is itching in my palms now. I'm try'nuh smack something proper," again growls the thug.

"Shit, who're you telling. I'm up early every morning."

"Al'ight. Say no more. I'm at the spot right now with a ripper slipper, but cold nympho. I'ma drop her ass off somewhere then get back in traffic. Meet me at Roscoe's on Main and Manchester in about thirty M's," orchestrates the thug. He's still tight over the liqk falling into someone else's hands after he'd been presented the opportunity to spank it himself. Just two weeks ago he and his crew had bumped into the coke head, Ron, at Rock & Reilly's bar in West Hollywood. And had he not just passed for a quarter mill on a different heist, he would have jumped quicker on the liqk. Oh well, shit happens.

"Al'right. Meet you at Roscoe's, in thirty. Mov'n!"

The thug disconnects the call.

HEART & HUSTLE

customized paint, burnt fire orange, convertible top CLS Mercedes Benz Coupe pulls into the lot and parks. Out climbs from the driver seat, a tall six foot stallion with long thick braided cornrows to the back and falling past her shoulders. She heads to the trunk and unloads a gym bag. Within several following seconds, the passenger door of this six figure cost, V6 turbo, luxury machine, opens and a second stallion almost as tall as the first exits. She looks around clueless about her surroundings, though well knowingly of her striking beauty that drips with sexiness. The light complexion of her skin is golden tan as a Sunkist.

"Where're we at, Six?"

"A gym," responds Miss Six, the tall six feet stallion.

Miss Six turns in a pair of open toe heels, closing the trunk of her car, and carrying bag in hand. She sports a tight fighting velour track suit that does nothing less than tease the stares she receives for having beauty, with a slim waist, and phat booty. The thighs and legs on her are as thick as a stallion's but pretty as a lady's. She's been compared to the body build of Serena Williams. Though not as masculine.

"What're we doing here; I thought that you said we had a meeting to attend about our hair product business?"

"We do, Orange'mist. And we're on time. Welcome to the corporate life. Meetings necessarily don't always take place in an office or conference room. You'll be surprised of how many important executives and other business types are meeting in gyms these days to discuss or negotiate plans and deals. So walk nasty, act classy, and play your A-game. Chipmunk is about to put us on."

Miss Six smiles at the thought of a new beginning. She had truly put her mind to it, to do it. Now she is a business woman. And Chipmunk is the businessman she has come to see. The two share history that runs deep from personally growing up in the hood together. Now it's hills with homes they each are growing on.

"But Miss Six, I'm dressed for a meeting. Not to be getting my fresh coochie all sweaty doing squats and calf raises. Or what not," playfully pouts Orange'mist. She sexily wears a business suit with heels.

"Girl, bring your country ass on. Don't worry. I have outfits in the bag he wants us to model in. To help market his business. That's part of the reason why we're meeting here. Anyways, it's time for a bad bitch to boss up another notch. And not for nobody else, but for our damn self. Let's go!"

Miss Six ends the small chatter and struts the way leading to the gym where she knows the opportunity to take her game to another level awaits her. At the ripe age of twenty-six, she has been hustling and in the hoe game now since she was seventeen. But only for the past six years has she been successful. It is how she bought the Benz that she drives, a two story brand new built town house with garage and pool that she lives in in Las Vegas, Nevada. And everything else she affords. All with cash. And all off a trick. Then now, too, she has Orange'mist. Her bottom bitch for the past two years.

Miss Six first bagged Toni, Orange'mist's original name, from a fake tennis shoe pimp down in Atlanta who didn't know what to do with her besides get her into strip clubs. Then with the money made they'd get high with or buy shoes and clothes. And when they ran through the money too fast, and a night wasn't lucrative on stage in the club, he'd have her set up tricks to rob. Miss Six came along, peeped game, maneuvered Toni away from the goofball, rechanged her name, gave her a different style, and then a new life. Ever since then, Orange'mists Phillipeno and Somalian ethnicity, multi-language speaking, short wavy hair, full breast, hazel eyes, and apple shape phatty has all been an asset. A large profitable one too. However, now it was time to use not only both their sex appeals, but too their brains to get a broader vision accomplished. In securing the bag for real.

Stanky Banky

After a thirty minute tread and light sweat, Chipmunk steps down from the treadmill and dabs his brow with a personal towel he owns that reads his brand's logo, draped around his neck. He sports a v-neck shirt and a pair of mesh fabric gym pants that each too advertise his company's brand: Fytness LyfeStyles. With a mission statement that reads: Youth Is In Having Gratitude For Fitness!

Dabbing sweat from his entire face now, Chipmunk stores a few mental notes away in his mind of the layout and atmosphere of the newest gym in L.A., Heart & Hustle. A place that has drawn the memberships of prominent people in sports, films and television, music, and corporate industry. But too including the common person. Over the past week, this is now the third gym he has visited for business research purposes. The first, being Gold's Gym Club. And second, L.A. Fitness. The plan is to open his own gym facility, but not prematurely. And so the bigger gym brands has become the scope and model of focus. Obviously because of his research: what attracts membership?

Chipmunk, a thinker before doer, one of patience, contemplates deeply in how to fuck this chicken lying before him. The vision he has is surreal. Already his brand is circling by word of mouth within prestigious social groups around L.A. and in other prominent regions throughout the nation. In several large retail stores, including Amazon's online platform, his brand's products: energy drinks and edibles, homebase fitness equipment, and now clothing apparel, are all on shelves.

Then there is the company's website that services to the health and lifestyles of adults, children, and pets. With personal fitness trainers, dieticians, veterinarians, life coaches, and treatment specialist all aboard to assist. All there is left now of his business venture goal is a gym facility. Or a compound with gym where clients can retreat to as a fun health facility with room and board; and undergo rehab recovery.

Another reason for Chipmunk being at the gym today is too to meet with a potential investor who's keenly interested in his business brand…

Miss Six and Orange'mist sashay into the gymnasium from the dress-rooms after changing, both looking apple biting seductive. However, their dress isn't provocative. But instead, has a jazzy look of taste. They each model a pair of drawstring gym shorts that are satiny in fabric, hug tight about the waist, but falls loose down around the midpoint of their thighs. Fully covering the buttocks, though setting free the bounce, shake, and giggle of it. Which Miss Six and Orange'mist has a whole lot of.

The two gorgeous amazons also sport open belly half tops, that are a combination of sports bra and tank top, thick stitched of the same material as the shorts. Their outfits are cute and colorful. Miss Six's dark ocean blue. Orange'mist's a sunny yellow-orange. Each with matching low ankle gym shoes. Fytness LyfeStyles is logo'd across the chest of their tops, and down the seam of the shorts. Though the mission statement reads different than stated on the apparel Chipmunk sports. Theirs read: 'Bread; Train 2 Go'…

Chipmunk sees and heads over to his potential investment: NBA Super Star, seven time All-Star, with a mean cross over then step back jumper that's both ugly but cash money, and who goes by the alias – The Beard.

He passes by, in route to his scheduled meeting, several women working out, some in enticing gym clothing. But pays their tight bodies no real attraction. A glance, but not a stare. He's a committed man. And unless another woman can be a valuable asset to him and his already existing family, a wife and eight-year young son, accepting the arrangement of a polygamy relationship, then he has no intimate interest in one at all. That's just how he's groomed and structured.

"What's up baller?" Chipmunk introduces himself with a fist pound and a back-shoulder slap. The ends of his braided hair dangle past his shoulders.

"Balling. How about yourself?" The Beard responds and returns the embrace.

"Balling is double standard with you. But off the court, likewise, I'm balling like a matha fucka," grins Chipmunk. He receives a gentleman's complimentary grin in return.

"Well look, you already know what the stats on the brand are. And also, what the current goal is. I received text that you and your people reviewed all of the paper work I forwarded you. So are we teaming up for a title?" Ask Chipmunk in a business tone.

"I know it might sound cliché of me, but I showed up to share the ball," smiles The Beard.

"Say no more. We're locked in: Fyt for Lyfe. And while you're dressed in the brand's apparel, let's go knock out this workout for the camera real quick. You know, for promotional purposes. I have everything already set up for us."

Chipmunk points The Beard in the direction of a private gym room he's preserved. And where several people await them to participate in the group work out he's orchestrated with camera crew. Taraji and Mary J., also members of the gym, are too scheduled to participate for the commercial recording. The marketing scheme for the brand is great. Especially now that a NBA superstar is the brand's ambassador.

At the exact same moment Chipmunk, with The Beard in company, turns to head for the awaiting session, Miss Six and

Orange'mist both walk up lady-like and business. The Beard does a double take in looking the two stallions over. So half does Chipmunk.

"Are they a part of the session?" The Beard, ask. Eyes glossy with lust and deeply set.

"Yes. But even better; team cheerleaders," answers Chipmunk while sharing a knowing smile of the eyes with Miss Six.

"And entrepreneurs," adds Miss Six. She holds the smile with Chipmunk, exactly the same, before then dropping her cat tight eyes on The Beard. Followed with a physical smile.

As if on cue, Miss Six and Orange'mist both lead the way to the private session room. The Beard follows first, mesmerized with Miss Six, but too on stand for Orange'mist. Chipmunk follows last, but not paying neither of the girls any mind. However, he still winds up locking eyes with Orange'mist. And for a second time now.

After the promotional workout session, and some light chatter once all were showered and dressed, Chipmunk later meets with Miss Six out in the parking lot of the gym. Orange'mist is still in company.

"So you ready to incorporate your heart and hustle?" Chipmunk gets straight to the business at hand.

"Yep. Me and my home girl here, Orange'mist, is ready. In fact, Orange'mist this is Chipmunk, and who I've been telling you about."

Chipmunk extends his hand for a proper shake. His gesture is met the same.

"Now you two have formally been introduced. But yeah, Chipmunk, me and my girl are looking to mass produce and market our hair care products. We've brought along some test kits to go along with our presentation."

"All right, say less. Explain the rest to Tracee EllisRoss. She's doing something similar already with hair care products for women with thick, curly, and coily hair. Her brand is called Pattern. I've set you an appointment with her that's in an hour from now. And tomorrow I have you scheduled with a lab and manufacturer here in L.A. to start the mass production. I'll personally help you market the product with my own marketing team." Chipmunk glances over at a T 50, V-12 that ice skates into the lot. A dream car of his priced at $2.3 million. He'll have one now sooner than later. He returns his attention. "I think you have something there with your shampoos and conditioners, et cetera. Or the better truth is, my 'wife' feels you have something here that's marketable. My investment in this will cover all cost to put the product out and help build your brand. So I'll handle to operation management too. You'll still remain C.E.O. and Founder of the brand. Deal?"

Miss Six smiles, but this time showing her pearly whites, and repeats "Deal". Orange'mist extends her hand to lock the deal in, but too finally speaks her sense in the matter.

"Please tell your 'wife' that we appreciate her being satisfied with our products. It means a lot. Maybe I can meet her someday." Again the lock of the eyes. But whatever it means, Chipmunk isn't caught in its trance. He's not the type to be easily persuaded or enticed. Especially not because a bad bitch locked eyes with him. Or shows interest. But at least it is clear to this bad, Phillipeno and Somalian, gorgeous looking pound cake, that he has a number one in his life already.

"Meeting my 'wife', that won't be easy. I don't let just anyone into my personal life. I take mines serious and with the upmost respect. But I'll be mindful to let her know that you two showed gratitude for her approval."

With that last bit said, Chipmunk tightly hugs Miss Six, whose eyes soften during the embrace, goodbye before hopping onto his Harley Davison sports bike and gearing off. The sound of loud exhaust pipes can still be heard a quarter mile distance after his departure.

83ʳᵈ STREET APARTMENTS

"A come in aunte, and close that gate. What's up; right here! I got you; what you need?"

A man straddling a Dymondback bicycle with his hair fro'd out beneath a white Houston Astro's fitted baseball hat, yells out to a kluk (crack head) standing at the gate of the apartment building looking to buy some work.

Inside of this two story, six unit, gated building, a crowd of gangbanging stars hangout under the sunny clear sky and good weather. Some of the men sport tank top muscle shirts while the majority a white-T pro club. Thick gold or bright platinum chains loop around the necks of a few, or single diamond stud earrings in their left ear lobe. And big face watches accommodate some of their wrists. Those not wearing any jewelry are either not on yet or doesn't find it necessary. However, they each still shine regardless because of the streets they roam: The Stanky Banky Eighties.

The kluk walks up to the man on bicycle after closing the gate shut behind her. She then digs over the collar and down into the shirt she wears to retrieve money she has stuffed into her bra. Quickly she pulls out several balled up bills and begins the process of straightening each of them out while too asking if she can get something for the $7 she has. By this time, the man on the bicycle has already dug down into his pants and boxers and retrieved a package containing crack rocks from the crease of his ass.

While this is all happening a blue Ferrari pulls onto the narrow block and parks along the curb directly in front of the apartment building. Out from behind the wheel climbs Tiny Trey Soljah dressed in long blue jean shorts, with a long sleeve blue shirt, both True Religion. And a blue pair of Chuck T's on his feet, with thick blue laces. On his crown he rocks a large 'T' Texas Rangers baseball fitted cap. A large blue diamond cut carat hangs from his left earlobe. It's the only jewelry he sports. Chains and watches aren't necessarily his thing. So for around his neck an orange, and a blue bandana, tied together at the ends hangs folded crease.

Tiny Trey Soljah bails through the gate into the apartment building, passes by the kluk coping work, then halts before several of his homies he greets and is greeted by. The one on the bicycle smiles then speaks.

"What's up, hoova boy. I see you boy."

"I see you too, Tiny Hoove. Still wrestling with these kluks and pulling crack out yo' ass. Huh, boyyy," Tiny Trey Soljah playfully jokes. Unintentionally he gets a few laughs from the crowd.

"What'eva. I take all the hooves, with yo' funny ass. And, I'm tapping on chins! What's up with yours?" Tiny Hoove grins while placing a stone into the kluk's hand in exchange for the $7. Quickly he replace the toilet paper wrapped package back in his ass.

"What. Watch out, groove!" Again smiles Tiny Trey Soljah.

However, Tiny Trey Soljah's response triggers the exact reaction he was looking to avoid with his beloved and reputable homeboy that played a part of his upbringing in the streets. Back when he first jumped off the porch and was initiated on the set at the age of fourteen, Tiny Hoove hand been a role model of his and an early mentor to him gangbanging and hustling. But right now he had just watch Tiny Hoove dig back and forth in his ass with crack. And so he was definitely not looking to play fight.

Tiny Hoove, leaving Tiny Trey Soljah no choice but to play, drops his bike and in a swift hop and step on his better leg, after years prior being wounded in the other, squares up on Tiny Trey Soljah who quickly throws his hands up ready to squabble. The two begin sparring and playfully slap boxing. A hood ritual.

Tiny Hoove good with his hands, catches Tiny Trey Soljah three to one in tapping each other's chin before stopping. They then embrace as they've always done. Slowly catching their breath. "You can't fuck with me, hoova. But, you looking groovy little homey," compliments Tiny Hoove while stealing a fourth tap to Tiny Trey Soljah's chin, who stiffens from the contact wishing he would have avoided it. But fuck it now.

"Yeah, you got me. I ain't tripping. Today the homey Baby Boy Blue H-day. Crim would've turned thirty-one. I just came from spending eighty three minutes at my rascal's grave," the thought stings him. "I woke up this morning and got banged up for groove. And for the lok little Blue Rag from Selo. But anyways, why're you on a cike. Where your hoop at?"

"Shit I'm always on a c'ike, hoova. No matter if I have three phat hoops; I'm in the set. But nah, my 760 Beamer parked in the back .My poundcake Brit, baby Cuppy, she somewhere in the new De'ville I got. That matha fucka phat too," boasts Tiny Hoove.

"Oh yeah, I seen one too. It is phat. G-Blac, who I be fucking with from Eleven-eight East Coast, got a money green one. You know they up right now. They 'G' homies Cake Head and Kiko just got out."

"Is that right. Shit, a lot of everybody homies that's been gone for a minute now home from the feds and state. That's why matha fuckas getting their sets back right. We all over here talking about that now. It's a bunch of more homies in the back," explains Tiny Hoove.

"Yeah I figured that. Plus Dragon and Little None text me

earlier and said the homies was deep over here. And I only see a handful up here. But before I slide to the back, is everything straight on that situation." Tiny Trey Soljah makes reference to the liqk he in turn put into Tiny Hoove's hands to execute.

"Everything smooth. The fence coughed up a ticket point nine for most of the jewels. The pieces that look to hold sentimental value is put up; waiting on you. Anyways, the five of us took two hun'nit stacks a piece. We hit all the loks locked up that we could think of with two stacks on their accounts. That was a hun'nit stacks. And with the rest of it, its set aside to invest with. What you and Chipmunk on, and how ya'll playing fair with the set, the homies can't help but follow suit and support the movement. At least as far as getting hooves and keeping the set right. The part about not beefing with the enemigos, everybody not receptive to that. We've lost too many to just let go, hoova. Feel me?"

"Yeah. But, the whole point of getting and keeping the set right is to stop losing. What's the use of having all this money and freedom today, if tomorrow we just going to get knocked down or get cracked for knocking something else down. That method defeats the purpose. We might as well stay broke and dusty. Fuck investing; fuck coping these phat hoops, houses; opening businesses, rocking jewels, or having children et cetera. That type of shit you live for to enjoy," Tiny Trey Soljah calms his tone that emotionally rises. He lets his youthful wisdom take lead. "Look, Hoove, there has to be a means to an end. Don't no war go on forever. So while we're on top and getting these hooves stanky banky, the Groove Line can control the momentum in the streets. Besides, the eighties is the heartbeat of the 'H'. If we lead by example, the rest will eventually follow. And I'm not saying that we start holding hands and singing Kum-by-yah with all those we beefing with, I'm saying cease fire. No different that when in the pen on the yard. We all black, first!" Tiny Trey Soljah expresses his mind from the heart. And is heard both emotionally and intellectually.

"I fell you, hoova. On hoova I do. And I'm with you groove. Come on, let's groove to the back. Now you have to make the same sense to everyone else. Hearing it come from a young reputable lok may change the way for the future you and Chipmunk want to bring forth."

Tiny Hoove leaves his Dymondback where it lays then he and Tiny Trey Soljah head to the back of the apartment building where over a hundred heads stand about speaking or listening to one another's opinion to gain agreements and structure.

CHIPMUNK

Chipmunk rides down the freeway exit ramp at the cross street, Florence Avenue, between Broadway and Figuroea Street. He slows to a stop behind a lane of vehicles held up at a red light. Back in the days, now fifteen years ago, he once walked or peddled bicycles along the streets of this neighborhood that has always been his home and, upon a time, homeless residence. Back then at these exit or entrance ramps around the inner city there would be a Mexican man or more than one, or Mexican woman, sometimes a small Mexican family, standing at the curb selling bags of fresh picked fruit: oranges, bananas, grapes, kiwi, or shell peanuts. But now he didn't see that anymore. The hustle or hunger wasn't the same. Or maybe it was simply that the era had changed.

The Harley breathes with a low growl idled in first gear still as he waits to kick it into second, then third and let the bike roar with speed. Back in the days as he too now recalls, barely twelve years old but already in the streets, then he was running from foster care homes and hiding from Children Services looking to take him back, to later absconding from boys group homes. Still, each and every time he was taken away he always made his way back home to his turf. And no matter how far away he was taken. The farthest had been three hundred miles and that still didn't deter him. During this time and phase of his life both his father and mother were in prison and serving long sentences exceeding twenty years, for armed bank robberies. And so the hood where he had already been born and raised, remained his home. Even after he became a ward of the state, he slept in abandoned houses or apartments, or sometimes in stolen cars to remain home. Though most times he was taken in by one of his older homeboys and they'd let him post up in a dope spot around the hood where he simultaneously learned how to sell drugs and make money. Even experienced his first blow job form a crack fein.

Gangbanging came with being a part of the streets. It was almost a certain than a choice for him. But too, his parents were Crips and so technically he was born into the lifestyle. However, and when at the age of twelve, he got officially put on his turf. And shortly after that he was putting in work. As many rightfully could have assumed then, his life was headed for destruction. Although, truthfully, in a sense, his life had been already a disaster. Up until his big homey Joe got a hold to him and cleaned him up: physically and mentally. Even cleansed his soul and spirit to a great degree.

The light changes green and traffic now begins to move turning right or left. Chipmunk takes a right and rides up to the second block where he then turns a left onto Hoover Street. He takes in the sight of his home and kingdom with joy. Although he no longer resides in this neighborhood of his, per se, not when having a two-story three bedroom Spanish Colonial, with back yard pool and patio, gated in a upscale community in the city of Chino Hills. Still the turf will always be his primary residence. Where now almost anyone will open their home to him as his own. Though a time before, many of the same people today, back in the day, would have told him to stay his troublesome ass away from their house, apartment, building, yard, or entire street. He laughs sometimes at the thought now.

But that was all then, and when he was entirely a gangbanging thug. Now today, he is a legitimate eight figure millionaire that owns prime real estate in four different states and two continents. And own or owns a share of equity in a variety of businesses ranging from clothing and shoe apparel stores to hair and beauty cosmetics supply stores; hair salons and barbershops; a record company; magazine and publishing company; a high-end rental agency for luxury cars and bikes to stock in a franchise food chain of restaurants. Then now his fitness brand and company. Which is projected to raise his net worth into the hundreds of millions. All is left of his mid-term achievements is to be a part of the uprise of his kingdom in the streets. Where he will always know as home.

Chipmunk turns into the T-shape alley off Hoover Street, in between the blocks of 83rd and 84th streets. He rides his bike through and parks it in the alley behind the 83rd street apartments. And is met by over one hundred of his homeboys, and a handful of homegirls but who aren't just the average type of homegirls. These are considered the 'lok Bitches' of the turf. He spots and acknowledge Ms. B, Lady Apples, Big and Baby Mickee, Lady SD, Peaches, Lady TC, Lady Astro, Mya, Trey Pop, and Lady Chipmunk a.k.a. Fe Fe just to name a few.

He slowly makes his way through the gathered crowd assembled in a meeting, he spots Tiny Trey Soljah; his lok of many to name. The two share the closest of bond together, dated back to his absconding abandonment days. Where they met, clicked, and since then have been inseparable.

TINY TREY SOLJAH

Tiny Trey Soljah stands surrounded by his clan and calls for their attention. Plenty of times before he stood in this same type of meeting, but didn't have a voice then; only a ear to listen with. Not just anyone can call for everyone's attention or voice their opinion and be heard in a meeting. Or surely not taken heed to. Both required for one to, first, have some level of respect or seniority, and or sometimes a backing of supporters. Which, second, all derive from having time in on the set and being in good standing. Since leaving home and running in the streets, he has shown nothing but real dedication to his turf and have always been in good standing.

Initially when he jumped off the porch into the streets it was a way of refuge from living in a single bedroom apartment with four of his siblings and their single parent mother. Which who's only source of income to provide clothing, shelter, and food came from county aid. His father didn't fare much in support.

He dropped by every now and then to help out, but had a separate family of five children and a second wife he lived with on the east side of town. Therefore it was little his father could provide when struggling himself, but ignorant enough to start families he later couldn't care for. A black man's self-inflicted struggle.

And so Tiny Trey Soljah took to streets to lighten the burden on his mother though not seeing how inadvertently it heavied her with anxiety over his whereabouts and safety. Still, and true, it was too late. The streets had quickly taken a hold of him. Then within no time after that, the lifestyle of gangbanging over came him. Back then it was either by choice or by force that an adolescent male teen be from a gang if caught roaming about in the streets. That's how it happened for him.

In his case it was by force. He'd turned up the wrong street one day and ran into a pack of rascals out roaming and lurking for trouble, or activity depending on who's point of view. Chipmunk was amongst the pack of mischiefs but had seen him roaming about solo a time or two before. This time there were no more passes. Chipmunk banged on him in asking what set he claimed. He answered he didn't bang but said it with a little too much base in his voice and Chipmunk T'd off on him. They then began squabbling right there at the corner of the street in broad day as though they were in a back yard somewhere, or boxing ring. Cars honked their horns, some stopped and watched, but most kept on about their own business. Then after he fought a good hard one with Chipmunk, a second member from the pack named C-Bang took him for a second round. Again, right there on the corner. And without getting much for a pause to catch his breath. Still, he didn't tuck tail or ever cry foul. Didn't even think to. Afterwards, and since that day, he and Chipmunk have been stump down together.

Early on, but now a member of a gang, he never had much but his name and good standing. Was dusty and grimy looking, though he developed a reputation to put in work. That's how he earned his name. But then his big homey Joe suddenly came along, pulled him up too, and dusted him off. Changing his life forever.

Tiny Trey Soljah begins by addressing the meeting with his vision to see the set rise, then his rational ideology for why. Which is again the same as he had moments ago expressed privately to Tiny Hoove. Reiterating the same question imposed: what is the purpose for striving, hustling, and all else to ball or survive today if the primary objective is gangbanging? And when the result of gangbanging equals to being in and out of jail, kill or be killed, and ultimately losing all across the board? Then he answers in part by expressing that that form of thinking will only continue to truncate their prosperity. By imprisonment or through early death. To make sure he's being understood and not just being heard, he elaborate his point to be made.

"It's like this groove. If we can sacrifice it all to gangbang, kill, take penitentiary chances, or die for one another; then we can make the same sacrifices to live, grow, ball, and remain free for another!" He holds his shoulders square, chin leveled high, and gives eye contact to as many as possible. "Listen. At some point you, we, have to change it up because every wave comes to an end. How I see it Crim, we can control the destiny of the streets. Or for sure in the set on Hoova Street! Some of the homies already on what I'm saying right now. And been on it way before me and Chipmunk woke up, stepped up our grooves, and got on it. But now it's time for the whole set to be on this same page. We're not just try'nuh see 'Da Eighties, Stanky Banky' and how Big Nasty use to say. We're try'nuh to see the whole 7-1-6 Stanky Banky. Like how me and the lok Chipmunk have incorporated Stanky Banky as a global enterprise, and a diamond medallion on chains. This shit simple like selling dope and striking on walls once you put your mind to it. If me and the lok can do it, and we came out the mud like you, cut from the same orange and blue cloths, then all the loks can. That means all of you." Again eye contact is held abroad. "Now as far as the enemigos go, many of them too are on what I'm conveying to you now. They're not try'nuh keep taking loses over the same shit going on fifty years now. But for those that are, they'll be the ones that get J.O.B.'d until they are erased! And even I will sacrifice it all to dead down the nigga-spirit in men so that the spirit of Ausar: God can live and grow."

Tiny Trey Soljah doesn't bother to look around to see the eyes of his comrades this time to tell whether or not his words are penetrating their minds, he knows that they are by their silence and patience with him. Besides, the message that he gives and his mentality that he portrays today isn't new to most who are present. They've heard the message before from another here or there. Besides, the new outlook he has on life they've all acknowledged for the past several years in how he grooves like a soldier that thinks. That much he demonstrates clearly.

"If anyone has any question or doubts just watch and follow my groove; I'll lead the way. After you catch on and or can lead us further, I'll then follow the lead. On Verz!"

Tiny Trey Soljah steps back, and from the center of the circle. He is commended by his comrades Lil Val, Trey Stone, Tiny Poke, and many others. His home girls Rosey and Misty both walk up and each gives him a hug filled with compassion for the love and dedication he shows. Then unannounced to him, Chipmunk walks from out of the crowd and pulls him back to the center of the crowd to stand side by side. The act seals trust and faith in all minds. Including those who secretly questioned or had doubt before about a change in direction and destiny.

ROSCOES'

The waiter walks up to the table occupied by three men and sets down two plates of waffles with fried chicken. The thug who had met and just finished dropping off the weed berry nympho that ate him up something decent, speaks to the waiter who's too a close acquaintance.

"Charles, is the register straight?" the thug asks.

"It's butter. But still put some bread in it while you got it. You know, it don't take much to melt a good thing. The best of diners can or have fell on hard times: M&M's, Bills Tacos, Ramona's. Anyway, Lil' G-Frog, before you leave stop in the kitchen and say hi to Ella. Today is her birthday."

"Oh, yea?" The three men sitting at the table all chime in in chorus. Then Lil G-Frog, the thug, digs into his pocket and pulls out a knot of money. He peels off four cenos and hands them over to the waiter. He, nor his comrade ever pay to eat at this place. Its apart of the hood.

"How old is aunte?" Lil –G-Frog inquires.

"Heck! I'm fifty-four. She's momma's oldest and that's at least six years older than me. But hey, how about you ask her when you go ta speak. See if she tells you or pop all the yellow off you with a frying spatula."

The table of men all chuckle a laugh, including the waiter before he leaves the younger men to their meals and privacy. Now alone to themselves again, they finish chopping game.

"Bosco, what was that you were saying about reading in the paper before Charles slid up?" Asks Lil G-Frog while biting into a waffle.

"After we hung up from the phone earlier, I finished reading the news paper before coming up here. Some matha fuckas clipped a museum in Boston for five million in art partings," reports Bosco, the man who Lil G-Frog called after seeing the report of the house heist on MTV news.

"Yum yum, gobble gobble." The third man at the table present breathes over a piece of fried chicken in hand, dripping with a bit of syrup.

"Exactly! Matha fuckas eating good; big chicken dinners," interprets Bosco of the third man's sound effects.

"Yeah, well, what' up with the next sting. Like you said earlier, it's on to the next one. You hear Tiny Squally hungry. And I'm thirsty," responds Lil G-Frog.

"Ain't no question. I'm trying ta' eat!" Second-motions Tiny Squally.

"Chill! I'm in the field doing my home work. Ya'll know how this shit goes. You got'ta let it fall in your lap. We're not rushing to the penitentiary behind being goofy; no matter how hungry or thirsty it get. Anyway, ya'll pushing with me to Vegas?"

"What's mov'n out there?" Ask Tiny Squally.

"Yeah, what's cracc'n!" Lil G-Frog persist.

Bosco takes and swallows a long gulp of sweet ice tea from the tall glass he's been nursing the whole time while the others ate. Now he holds the glass out in front of him and looks at it for a second as though a light has went on inside it.

"Starz. What else are we talking about. The bag is not just here in L.A. It's everywhere: omnipotent. That's why I be everywhere: omnipresent. The law of attraction sometimes pulls you. And when it does, wherever it pulls you to you go. You never know where the bag may fall into your lap or who you run into: omniscient. So are ya'll coming or not!"

STEADY SCHEMING ~ THA PLAYBOY KILLA

"Here, honey. Try this on. This will look grandish on you. Sir, wouldn't you agree?"

The snow fox, draped in a pink floral strapless Richard Quinn $3,000 dress with matching $1,300 pink pumps and a $5,000 pink designer hand bag purse, points to a wall of high-end men's coats and jackets and picks out an expensive $13,000 fur and leather Dolce & Gabbana jacket. The store-host glows in agreement with the selection, then quickly helps this seasoned Armenian woman with expensive taste and class; and that strikingly favors Chris Jenner by looks. Together they take the jacket down from its rack to then hand to the woman's younger black male stud in company. Since he and lady come into the All Saints store she has charged up twenty grand already: purchasing a Marc Jacobs peacoat, a Polo sports jacket, and a Tom Ford suit coat. Now with this new purchase to tack on, commission is looking sweet for the host/retailer.

Male'Rose a.k.a. Tha Playboy Killa, the young stud, walks over from viewing a glass show case of watches a short distance away and gives his undivided attention. He sports a tailored pair of gray slacks, a dark blue Hermes crew cut, body fitting, shirt that snug's his muscular physique and that color coordinate with a pair of croc leather Hermes shoes on his feet, and a $1,200 Hermes belt about his waist. To further accommodate his taste and style he peers from behind a pair of expensive Hermes shades and checks the time on the $46,000 Audemars Piguet (AP) clasped around his wrist.

"Hand the jacket to the lady, will you!" Male'Rose politely orders.

"Why certainly, sir." The host ~ retailer oblige and free his hands from the jacket the lady still partially holds.

"Now go ahead babe; dress me in your vision." Male'Rose commands.

The snow fox gladly takes and opens the jacket for Male'Rose to put his arms through, then helps pull the jacket up over his shoulders while she stands before him in cheer.

"You look very handsome, dear. Please, I must buy you this also. May I?" Male'Rose turns to his left and looks himself over in a full body mirror before turning back to his mistress. He plants a kiss on the bridge of her nose. Her favorite spot.

"I endure your taste. Yes you may."

Male'Rose then grabs his mistress's hands and squeeze them gently. The snow fox blushes red then turns to the retailer.

"Sir, can you kindly charge this purchase also to my card. Thank you."

"Yes ma'am. Anything else, sir?"

Male'Rose grins to himself first, before acknowledging the host's acknowledgement of him having a rich bitch gladly spending a bag on him. In reply, he press two fingers together then taps them to the brow of his head in a gesture of salute. No words included. Understanding the silent language, the host spins on his heels with black card in hands and goes to ring up the final purchase.

However, the before hand gesture in Male'Rose squeezing the

snow fox's hands, was a silent que that the purchase would be the last. He doesn't want to trigger a red flag although he and his cougar both feel completely comfortable about their actions.

The snow fox is a madam of the white collar game and on all levels of it. She has banked in multi-millions of dollars, properties et cetera. And still counting. But now she only does what she has mastered, when she does so every now and then, just to be bashful. It's another way for her to let her hair down. But too, to stick it to the feds who once got their hands on her now over ten years ago. They kept her canned for twenty months on a thirty months sentence for money laundering and tax fraud. That's how Male'Rose wind up knocking her, while they both were locked up at the MDC building in downtown, Los Angeles. He was in on a charge for counterfeit money and had seen her on an attorney's visit. He spoke in passing, got a smile out of her, but later wrote her a kite and had it sent up to the 9th floor where she was housed at. And from pen pals passing time, to friends, and now lovers they became.

Outdoor of the mall plaza a burgundy, dark window tinted, Jag truck on 22" Forgees pulls into receiving of the mall's valet parking. The valet driver exits from behind the wheel and holds the door open for the snow fox who finishes off a martini seated beneath a umbrella table.

Male'Rose takes a call while climbing into the reclined passenger seat of the Jag and his lady takes the wheel. The valet driver loads the shopping bags neatly into the rear of the truck. And the snow fox later tips him.

"Wesst," answers Male'Rose into his phone.

"What it do bro. Where you at?"

"In traffic with my top piece. Just left the Delamo; on that 'just throw it in the bag!', shit."

"Is that right; so what's up. I heard about the sliders, they sliding like that?"

"A-1 bro. What's up tho'?" Male'Rose cuts to the point.

"Shittt, I'm trying to catch up with you and grab one with about fifty on it."

"Twenty-five bands; I'll be coming down Rosecrane in a second. You got yo' weight up or do you need to holla back in a couple weeks when you do. I'll be back from Vegas in a few days," smiles Male'Rose shooting a shot jokingly.

"You got me fuuuucked up, loc. Pull up. On the set, money stanky in the Gunz. Slide down a hunnid and thirty-fif'. I'm in Gardena now."

"That's a bet." Male Rose disconnects the call.

Fifteen minutes later the Jag truck pulls up on 135th and Crenshaw. A all white new 760 BMW on 23" Lexonys is parked in the drive way of the house the Jag stops before. A stocky built man wearing a muscle tank top with tattoo block numbers on his biceps, sporting a pair of blue khaki shorts and blue corduroys house shoes on his feet, walks out from the house to the Jag. He tosses Male'Rose a Crown Royal Velour bag stuffed with cash in exchange for a credit card with a $50,000 charge limit. Thirty seconds later the Jag pulls off.

A block away Male'Rose receives a text: 'Cuz you stay in something phat. But the snow fox; on Gunz, was that Chris Jenner?' Male'Rose smiles at the compliment. It's a brag to pull up with a young bad bitch in the passenger seat that'll hop out and stall traffic by just her looks. But to pull up with something gorgeous in her fifties or older and that has a bag, driving behind the wheel of something foreign, and you're a intellectual lok navigating directions from the passenger seat, is being smooth on another level.

Male'Rose texts back: 'SLM'F (Smiling like a matha fucka). Nah lok, this not her. But on Verz, I'm steady schem'n!'

CRUSH GROOVE: PRIVATE AND INDUSTRIAL SECURITY INC.

Elevator doors open on to the third floor of a downtown, seven floor, office building. The biggest pop star diva of the year exits into a nicely furnished den of a reception lobby with her dad and personal body guard. A set of stainless, floor to ceiling, glass doors open from the lobby into two thousand square feet of floor space converted into ten office cubicles coupled with two large private offices that each have a single tinted window that sees out but not in. The same is for the conference room twenty feet from the lobby doors.

At this hour of the morning the office cubicles are busied with its ten employees who each are either answering phone calls, receiving or sending faxes, typing or scrolling away on desk top computers, but all dealing with clients' security travels, home security, private personnel request, and general questions or concerns.

Out from one of the two private offices that both face the lobby and floor space, appears a stocky built man with a nicely trimmed grey haired goatee, bald shaved head, sporting a immaculate Steve Harvey suit, named Chip. He greets his newly arrived guest, soon to be clients, ushering through the lobby's doors by one of his company's security personnel.

Over inside the conference room awaits the puzzle master behind it all, dressed in a suit jacket with jeans. He's accompanied by his business associate, Maxi, who he met back when she was in college now nearly a decade ago. She runs one of L.A.'s top publicist companies. Not to mention who's also the vice president of one of the hottest magazines published in the nation: The West Report. In fact, her name and association throughout the entertainment industry is what helped assemble the present meeting. The two now stand from sitting in two of several lush office sofas circled around a small table several feet away form a large conference table. They were enjoying casual conversation with laughs when the arrival of their guest enters the room. Instantly Maxi and the Pop star hug in greeting each other. She greets the father the same, who is also the singer's manager. She's well acquainted with them both. And now she makes the introductions.

"Well I see you've already met Edmond aka Chip, so let me have the honor of making the second introduction here. Britney, this is my dear friend and business associate Christopher Heru."

"Please, you may call me T.S. as do everyone I befriend," interjects the puzzle master extending his hand to the pop star diva, her manager, then personal body guard.

After the friendly and formal greetings are made, Chip recenter's the primary focus of the meeting at hand. Business.

"O.K. ladies and gents, lets now discuss the reasons for why we are here. Afterwards we can all do a late lunch together, if our schedules permits so," he waves the group over to take seats at the conference table. "Ms. Britney, the services of Crush Groove Private and Industrial Security can assure you one thousand percent, special detail in providing an air tight system of security. The same as this company provides for all of our clients." Chip's entire demeanor affirms he stands behind his words. "Now we understand that a house of yours was broken into last month and valuables, still not recovered, were taken. Our service can help prevent a second incident from ever happening again."

"Please, may I interject," interjects the puzzle master. Seeing that it is perfect to get straight to the set up.

"To add to my uncle's representation of our company, acquiring our services not only safeguards your home and values, possibly return some of what had been taken from the recent theft. But also, I assure you 'complete comfort' when in the city of Los Angeles. That I stand on one thousand and eighty-three percent!"

The pop star diva swallows her saliva, then tongues the sudden dryness of her mouth. The situation before her makes her feel somewhat cornered. But the circumstances of it affirms her actions. "Yes, I'm fully aware. That is why I am here; Mr. Trey Soljah."

ORANGE'MIST.

"Girl, what're you writing. You've been in here all night?"

Miss Six stops and leans into the door frame of the open bedroom. Her body is wrapped in a bath towel from chest down, though just barely covering her peach tree between her thighs while the bottom of her wagon out back bounces freely. Her hair, now styled straight, is tied back in a long pony tail. Partially still wet, she holds a iPhone in hand.

"I was just finishing up a chapter in my book I'm writing about my life," answers Orange'mist. She lays across the top of her bed on her stomach in nothing but a cherry thong and small v-neck t-shirt that reads, Fytness LyfeStyles.

"Now, I'm beginning a new chapter. Why, what was you doing?" she asks but still focused on her writing.

"In the shower entertaining my OnlyFans page. I was now walking back on my way to my room and noticed the door open and you still in here. In ten minutes I'll be ready to finish up the last show for the night. Tonight's theme is: Cream-me-good-night." Miss Six giggles then turns to leave.

"Wait!"

Miss six turns back, and without trying to her ass cheeks clap sounding still wet.

Orange'mist rolls over from her stomach and sits up straight, with her legs spread out in front of her. She arches back on her hands, palms down on bed, and her chest heaves forward.

The nipples of her large breast, beneath the fabric of the shirt she wears, look the sizes of small thumbs on a baby. And her thick thighs align with the sides of her bottom that spill out beneath her. Miss Six looks her over skeptically then answers, "What!" with emphasis.

"Bitch please; strictly dickly. I just want to share some thoughts with you for feedback," answers Orange'mist reading the bewildered look on Miss Six's face. Bumping pussy was definitely not her thing!

"Okayyy, I did ask 'what?' before jumping to conclusions. I ain't trying to turn you out on the new norm. But you are in here with your nipples hard and all."

Unaware of the observations just made. Orange'mist quickly looks down and takes notice of her breast. Her nipples are on stand; perky. Then now she suddenly feels the moisture between her tights. Shyly she brings her legs in together and cross her ankles. Hoping that Miss Six hadn't noticed her coochie wet also.

"I told you I'm in here writing," she defends.

"Yeah, but who are you in here writing or thinking about is the point." Miss Six stares at Orange'mist closely, half knowing the answer to her own question.

"I didn't say anything about a person. But anyways, I'm thinking about the start of a new chapter in my life to go along with this new chapter in my book. Well actually let me rephrase that because the new chapter in my life has already begun. But to stop it from turning out the same as anything prior, I have to let go of a few old ways so that it doesn't interfere with, or possibly prevent, this new phase in life that actually me and you both are coming into," her eyes brighten with cheer then slowly dim with anxiety. "Miss Six, if our hair products grow really big as a business then we're talking about millions of dollars. That means we can really change our lives. We don't have to deal with tricks anymore, pop our ass and coochie for dollars, or be on web cams running entertainment sites for perves. Girl we can retire and live normal lives. Right?"

Orange'mist now looks at Miss Six with strong enthusiasm before looking down and away. She knows she isn't the dominant of the two.

Miss Six, still with iPhone in hand, now stands up straight and places her hands on her hips presuming the dominant role. "Nope, bitch! Because the truth is you now all of a sudden think you want a boyfriend or to be the second wife in a polygamist marriage because you then fell your ass in love with the thought of being with Chipmunk's high yellow ass. Keep that shit real! You've been all goofy in the head ever since I introduced you two. But it's understandable; what boss bitch wouldn't want, or hasn't at least once fantasized about, a 'real' dominant man that can please her and make her feel even extra secure. Even I have," her shoulders square in facing Orange'mist. Her tone now bossy.

"However, don't get it twisted. As a woman you will always deal with a trick of some type when trying to get something done or accomplish anything great in this American male, and now dyke, driven society. Because the biggest of tricks are at the tops of this corporation and running it with their horny asses. And therefore, that ass and pussy is going to pop for dollars, power, or position regardless if you want it to or not; if you want power, wealth, or position. Hell, too, if you plan on keeping a partner that's faithful to you. Or else a bad boss bitch like me is gon' run him for that check he suppose to bring home. Once you start getting fat, sloppy, ass loose and flat, don't want to do this or that anymore, and you're now completely busted because you've then fell off your game thinking shit sweet." Mix Six pause to let the truth settle.

"Now another thing, since you've brought it up! When, not if, our hair products start running that bag up in the millions of blue faces, you can choose to live whatever life you wish to. I support you. Just don't fall off all the game I'm teaching you. I may not be there or able to scoop you up a next time! Oh, and if you plan on being anything marital to Chipmunk then understand this—over half the game I got, I learned from him. So game will recognize game."

Miss Six turns on her heels to leave but then stops and speaks over shoulder. Her back now to Orange'mist.

"By the way, your OnlyFans page show starts ten minutes into mines for Thursday's 'double treats'. So go ahead and get your mind right and focused on what's right now! You're not rich yet, bitch."

Orange'mist falls flat onto her back after Miss Six has long since disappeared to her own room. She inhales a deep breath then lets it out slowly. "Not yet," she repeats to herself and dismisses the thought of Miss Six. Her hands then run over her breast, stopping to massage her nipples still hard, before trailing down below and underneath the fabric of the thong. She smiles to herself at how wet she feels. Then the image of Miss Six quickly reappears. "But soon, bitch!" she says aloud before the image of Chipmunk instantly returns and turns her faucet fully on. Now she's ready and focused for what's necessary, right now!

LAS VEGAS

L ight-cameras-actions-ballers lets get ready to play/ we're on the strip. Where them gangstas dip/ and kill you for anything/ I know – I- want-to see myself with-major-thangs/ but I also want to see my kids/ to know their daddy.'
"Cut!"

The director yells on set. She is the hottest female music video director in the game, and right now she just finished directing the music video to the hottest song in the streets out West and climbing the Top 40 Billboard chart in the nation entitled, 'Let's Get Ready 2 Play.'

"Good looking out baby momma. We're gon' put the West on the map with this one," smiles Male'Rose of his video shoot.

"Boy stop playing before you have some kids for real."

The two laugh and dap each other up showing nothing but love. The video set is still lit with models, exotic and foreign cars, gang stars from all over – both men and women – who showed up for support and to be featured in the video. The same for a couple casino bosses who made an appearance to help liven the skit.

Moments later and while the crowd still hangs loose, a 63' Chevy Impala, fire orange candy painted on 13" one hundred spoits rounds the bin set up and stops out front of the dressing trailers on set. Male'Rose steps out from one of the three trailers designated for him; one for the director, and the other for the models.

"Wesss. What it do next?" Shouts Male'Rose, still feeling in the moment of natural stardom. His album is scheduled to drop next.

"T.S. scheduled the photo shoot with the boy, Ron. He's out here too. So let's knocked that out the way. But first, I'ma put this up on the rack to have taken back to the land; jump back in the Raith and then we can pull up to the Mayfair Supper club at the Bellagio. I'm hungry as fuck," the thought on second thought intensified the hunger. "I have a table reserved. Plus I told Ron to meet us there already," announces Chipmunk from behind the wheel of his toy classic brought out and featured in the video.

"Say less. I'm waiting on you." Responds Male'Rose

Stanky Banky

"Eww. What the fuck is this you have us eating?"

"I don't know what cuz talking about, this shit smacking," interjects Tiny Squally. He stabs a fork back into his plate of food, greedily. Ignoring Lil G-Frog.

"It's smoked salmon covered in spicey apple cider sauce. And that there is cooked Brussel sprouts. Rich man eating. Not them sloppy ass hamburgers or chili cheese fries with pastrami you use to eating at Tam's or Burger Palace. Or eating chicken and waffle every day," explains Bosco to Lil G-Frog.

"Hold up! I don't know what you talking about now. Them chili cheese fries with pastrami be smacking. On Gangstas!"

"That's a fact! I eastside 'G' that," stamps Lil G-Frog.

"Yeah you would east side 'G' some shit like that with your easty ass. Both of ya'll need to start getting outside of the hood more often to try different shit: food, events, people, and some real bad bitches —"

"What, like them?" Interjects Lil G-Frog. Through the restaurants window he looks and points out two stallions, drop dead gorgeous, who have just pulled up the Bellagio and climbed out of a money green Bentley Bentayea brand new off the lot. The ladies each sport romper dresses with nice matching sandals and jewels glistening off of their sexy bodies.

"Yeah, you can definitely 'G' that," agrees Bosco. "But peep! Look who we just ran into on a humbug coming through the door; 9-o'clock. See how shit fall in yo lap. Ya'll done smacking."

❖   ❖   ❖

Stanky Banky

"Hi. Yes, I'm one of several patrons reserved for a table for five under the company name, Stanky Banky Entertainment."

"Let me check please," the hostess flips open a booking bill and scrolls down the list of reserved tables. Then stops mid-way. "Yes. And it is precisely 2'o'clock. This way, sir. I'll have a waiter show you to your private V.I.P. section and table."

Ron, wearing a pair of dark tint bottle cap designer frames and dressed casual, still having that incognito air to him, follows the waiter to his table. The waiter then hands him a menu before leaving, but promising to return on call.

Not five minutes after the waiter has departed, Ron receives company. Bosco, Lil G-Frog, and Tiny Squally all take seats at the table drawing no attention. He could use a distraction right now to help ease out of this certain confrontation he's not cut out for one bit.

"What're you looking around for Ron; What, you didn't expect to see a gangsta?" Lil G-Frog mugs Ron without blinking.

"Say brothas, I don't want no smoke. Business is business. I haven't done anything against any codes you guys live by."

Nervous, Ron stutters on a few of his words while worrisomely keeping his cool. He has a good idea what this run down on him is about and thanks his lucky stars that the encounter is happening in a public setting with plenty of witnesses around.

"Who accused you of anything. We just stopped by to congratulate you on the handoff up the middle. That was a nice score. But now since you're feeling guilty, we do need some of them starz you counted. Like A-sap!"

Bosco leans in on Ron from across the table to put emphasis on his light press. It works.

"Whoa, whoa, wait a second man. You're meaning money, correct? Stars? Hey I didn't score but five grand up front on that info. I'm waiting now to pick up double that, maybe a little more. But surely nothing like I assume you guys are thinking. I swear. And I only went with someone else after you didn't get back up with me. I called and left messages. I swear —"

"Hold up! And fuck all that you called me shit. You only touching fifteen to twenty bands from that liqk," Lil G-Frog couldn't believe what he just heard. But then again he could, on second thought. He would have given the coke head less than that. Now he's even more madder he didn't take the advantage to.

"Who did you pass that liqk to?" He ask before being interrupted —

"What's good Ron; What's all this? Wes' happn'n homey?"

Chipmunk walks up, speaks to Ron for clarity. But then bangs on Lil G-Frog, Bosco, and Tiny Squally for recognition seeing that they were unfamiliar gang starz. And, not invited guest at his table.

The crew sitting immediately stand from their seats and hold their ground against the unexpected arrival of Chipmunk and Male'Rose. Then simultaneously faces, with names to them, between both side start to relocate. And instantly animosity flares. Back in the days they had gang beef as rivals. It could still be same now.

"Tiny Squally, what's smooth?" Male'Rose bangs.

"Back-West, Northside Mov'n, cuz! What's cracc'n?" Tiny Squally bangs back.

"Strictly Groov'n!" Chipmunk stamps with a stump of his

feet.

"Eastside Mov'n," counteracts Lil G-Frog before he's quickly cut off.

"Hold up! Fall back G-Frog and Squally. We're not out here for that. What's up Chipmunk and Male'Rose, we not doing no set tripping this far in the game. Ya'll getting hooves and we're counting starz. Everybody getting to the bag now. So is it a issue?" Bosco, wisely using reason, quickly speaks up to hopefully diffuse what can surely blow up. He's also the lessor active gangbanger among him, Lil G-Frog, and Tiny Squally. But only because of his maturity today and his success in life derived from being so.

"Listen lok. This our table reserved, for one. Then two, the way the boy was sitting here looking when we walked up, like if ya'll was over here pressing him about something. That's cool, but you gon' have to do it somewhere else. And, catch him a later time because right now he's on my time," strongly affirms Chipmunk.

Everyone now looks down at Ron who is glued to his seat but now with his chin in his chest and twirling the thumbs of his hands held finger-interlock.

"You know what, I respect that loc. And on some 'G' shit, my bad. We've been hearing about ya'll corporate thugging, too. Real recognize real all day," commends Lil G-Frog.

"I 'G' that too, as a man," second-motions Tiny Squally.

"Don't trip. It's all our bad. Both sides have to wake up from this deep sleep. And since we're chopping it up real quick, it'll be appreciative if you let those know on ya'll sides of the land that our side is on this Stanky Banky shit. Unless provoked to be on the bullshit. And if it get to that, then we're J.O.Bing to erase shit off the map!" Promise Chipmunk, with a $200,000 Stanky Banky medallion hanging on a shiny bright chain still around his neck since the video shoot. The exact same with Male'Rose.

Without any further words exchanged between the separate sides, Ron's extorters start to leave from the table and relieve him of the momentary fear they caused. Plus too all the unwanted attention and stares from others dining at tables nearby caused by the small confrontation. But now suddenly, the two stallions appear – causing their own scene.

"O.K. baby. I salute it. And no disrespect locos, this ya'll?" Ask Bosco while giving Miss Six and Orange'mist both compliment stares.

"Shit, shoot your shot. We're just doing business for my photo shoot later," grins and chuckles Male'Rose. Recognizing a gangsta with mack in him.

Bosco takes heed while too stepping aside for the ladies to take their seats. He caps at Orange'mist who is closest to him. His comrades freeze up, both intimidated by the class and beauty of these two bad bitches their not accustomed to bagging. However, Orange'mist declines to give her attention.

"I'm sorry dear, but I wouldn't be good company. My entire mind and feelings are completely consumed by the thought of someone else." Orange'mist takes her seat then sets her full attention on Chipmunk.

HEADQUARTERS

I seen the commercial ad. It's been running all week. That's a good look with the 'Beard' on board. In fact, a contact of mines just hit me today and says his client is feeling the brand and is now inquiring; wants to meet up to see what's possible. Sees the vision in the brand being bigger than Jenny Craig or anything else out there. Anyways, the meeting is up to you. It can't make or break us. But now guess who he works for?" Asks Tiny Trey Soljah.

He and Chipmunk shoot a game of pool inside a downtown loft they share overlooking the city through floor to ceiling glass walls on it's lower deck. The place is plushed in the likes of an exotic bachelor pad slash office. With high-end cost furnishing and tech appliance, Art painting and sculptors further decorate the main floor. While a fifty gallon fish tank, swimming with exotic fish sets off the upper deck with awe. The place is their private resort in the city, and used as a 'think' tank. Here is where they find solace and chop up game.

"Who. The homey Kawhi, or Candice Parker? Or La'Bron, since he's out West now?" Guesses Chipmunk but without much enthusiasm.

"Those'll be a good look too; but nah. This person don't even play sports. And my contact is not a agent or PR. He does hair. He's Kim K's personal stylist."

Chipmunk stalls in taking his next shot on the table and looks over at his 'day one' with a screw face.

"Do hair? What's up lok; where've you been hanging out at on the down low? Don't get d.p.'d, Crim."

"Watch out. You got me fucked up, hoove. Only thing hanging down low about me is these nuts," smiles Tiny Trey Soljah at Chipmunk's cheap shot taking jokingly.

"But for real tho', dude is straight. He just fuck with hair. And he's checking a bag for like eighty bands a year just from Kim alone."

"Damn, that's what's up. But as for Kim, you can line it up. I'll hear what she's talking about. You know I respect Kanye on that far out shit he be on; but most not catching. Anyways, what's up with the label on your end of business. What's the next move?"

Chipmunk lines his shot up again and finally takes it. He knocks in a stripe. Now he screens the table for his next shot.

"The R&B artist you signed, buzz is growing. He opens up for SZA tonight; in about an hour. Aside from that we're still negotiating Ella Mai out of that bogus contract she's in so we can then sign her to Stanky Banky and start recording. I got Hit Boy, who's sizzling right now as a producer, ready to work with some of our artist and get in the studio with Ella Mai on our behalf. But who she's still signed to is in his feelings. Shit gon' get political if this next phone call not sounding right. And gon' turn something into ketchup and mayonnaise. Now I see why Suge was on some gangsta shit with these squares. Whinnies be playing tough if you let' um." Tiny Trey Soljah speaks while too closely observing the table for Chipmunks best shot. "But other than all that, shit smooth. Matha fuckas paying their dues to Crush Groove. We apply comfort and security to twelve percent of the industry now. Then you already know the math with the lok Male'Rose. His singles out are all in the top 100 on the billboard, and his album is basically done and ready. Besides that, a couple dimus from Family's looking to get signed. A cat from Neighborhoods that can sing and flow try'n to go if we're not tripping. I told him it's all about how he carry it. We black before orange or powder blue. And the money today have big blue faces, so there's common ground. He get the point. But yea, they're all going to be at the club tonight I just mentioned trying to be signed. All their music go too. I have them booked as our acts tonight. After we see their performances, we can chop it up from there."

Chipmunk agrees with the operations of the record label and Tiny Trey Soljah's train of thought. Now he takes his next shot and misses poorly. But knocks in a solid color ball.

"Don't help me; help the lions, tiger, and bears," tease Tiny Trey Soljah before he rounds the table twice then halts to take a favorable shot.

"Yeah you got that. But let me bring up something real quick while its best to speak on it now," suddenly announces Chipmunk. "I ran into a few opps out in Vegas the other day for the video shoot. And they had a squeeze on the boy, Ron. Groove was shaking like the ass cheeks on Prince performing at a Purple Rain concert."

Tiny Trey Soljah pauses from taking his shot and chuckles a laugh.

"Na'h for real! The boy was spooked." Chipmunk resumes with saying.

"Yeah I know. He ran back to me crying for protection," informs Tiny Trey Soljah.

"I'm not feeling a good vibe, hoove. Also, before me and Male'Rose pushed up on our table where they had him pressed – I believe he coughed up who he gave the play to. And if he didn't, he will. Especially if them people snatch him up," warns Chipmunk.

"Say no more. Its understood!" Agrees Tiny Trey Soljah.

"That's a bet. But look, let me clean up. I need to run something through the field to see if its built to last."

"Yeah I heard about that too; indirectly. Male'Rose mentioned the photo shoot. Anyways, you sure?" Questions Tiny Trey Soljah for certainty. The wheels in his head pause from quickly turning in how he himself planned to clean up if left to him.

"Yeah I got it. My lok Bitch gave me the signal. And you know how we slide, J.O.B x H.O.G!"

"Say no more. Lets head out now and go put on for the medallion on the chain," concludes Tiny Trey Soljah.

"On Verz; Stanky Banky. Lets groove!"

HOUSE OF BLUES

A fleet of ten exotic and foreign luxury vehicles ranging from a trio of Bentley Bentaysa v-8, a trio of Bentley Raiths, to two Lambos, and two fully loaded H3 Hummers on 30" Blueface-bussums each, all pull up in caravan out front the most historical venue for music and performance in a night club know in L.A. The night's club attendances are lined from the door to the end of the block and all watch in astonishment as Stanky Banky Entertainment entourage make their presence felt.

After parking in reserved stalls, the party of twenty-five mob to the front entrance ignoring the waiting line. And without delay the entire party is let in then shown to their V.I.P section where bottles of Champagne await them in buckets of ice at each table.

Other celebrity guest in attendance show love or admiration to the Stanky Banky crew, sending either their greets or a complimentary bottle of champagne throughout the night. And Chipmunk's signed R&B artist gives a stella performance for opening act. Then SZA performs and shuts the stage down. The crowd goes up the whole entire night coupled with all the other performances. And members of Top Dog Entertainment slide through V.I.P and pop bottles with Stanky Banky.

Although the night is lit, it doesn't end without static. Most in attendance came out to have fun and enjoy a memorable evening of music, dress, and performance. However, amongst all are a few camouflaged in and lurking for a come up...

"Say, where's the restroom. I got'ta take a leak?" Asks a member of the Stanky Banky entourage.

"Come on, this way. I'll push with you. My bladder heavy too from all this Ace of Spade," replies Male'Rose. He and his homeboy then slide off duo together.

The men's room is full, and there is a waiting line outside its door. Male'Rose and his homeboy grow frustrated but they decide to head out to the parking-lot to use it for convenience. In between cars they each finally relieve themselves...

Five men lurking lag behind in following Male'Rose out of the club and into the parking lot. The icy Cuban lynk chain and Stanky Banky medallion around his neck is too much not to snatch. That's a $200,000 piece; not including the cost of the chain. They had been seeing him previously with it on all over Instagram and in UTube music videos. Plus, Kite magazine, straight stuntin, Viro magazine, and The West Report all have featured him with it. Tonight when they spotted, not one, but three of these Stanky Banky medallions in the club hanging on platinum Cuban lynks or blue diamond stud chains and around the necks of their now target, Tiny Trey Soljah, and Chipmunk each respectively, it was far too much shine not to get some of it. Though having it wouldn't have came easy until Male'Rose strayed away from the pack...

Two of the five men enter the parking lot first, while three hang back at the entrance but making as if they have stepped outside for a casual smoke, though secretly are watching the walkway form the front door of the club to the parking lot. However, anyone passing by can smell the bomb bud in the air.

The two jackers, now clearing the gap between them and target, unexpectedly pass by a couple out too using the parking lot for convenience. The rear door of a small car hangs open and the lower half of a woman's petite body bends out with her skirt up around the waist, as she's sprawled out across the back seat. Behind her, and hitting her doggy style, stands a man with his pants down around his ankles. He pounds away while gripping a handful of her ass cheeks. The couple are completely unaware or can give a damn about being noticed, and so the jackers move along as must have Male'Rose and his homeboy…

Male'Rose zips up just as two masked men approaches him. The jackers waste no time upping hammers while a third masked man runs up in the same pursuit with his hammer out. Male'Rose's homeboy, startled, hurries with zipping up but then stands his ground beside his homeboy.

"Time to spread the wealth and come off that chain for sagging like if this couldn't happen," barks one of the three gun men. Relieved that the men running down on them isn't over gang related beef, because had it been so then surely the guns aimed on him and his homeboy would have blazed with no regards for the chain, Male'Rose exhales through his nose while keeping a poker face.

"You got it. And I'm not fucked up about it. The only thing is, these hands of mine are not gon' peel myself. One of ya'll gots to do that. I ain't tripping."

As Male'Rose makes his statement, a dark SUV speeds through the parking lot in reverse coming to a stop before the group. Out from the passenger seat a fourth member of the jacker crew jumps out. With a cannon in hand.

"What, he try'na to get dirt nap'd over this shit?" The man growls.

"Nope! Just hurry up and grab the chain off his neck. And don't break it! Snatch that icy shit off his wrist too. And ya'll two, go in their pockets. Stump quick! We out in 'eight' seconds," orders the leader. The one who's done the only talking out of the first three.

The leader also sees in his peripheral three women come into the lot headed to a car but unaware of the liqk going down. No need in making a scene not warranted. His pistol for all of his career has cocked and aimed for the money, not for killing. And this just went sweet for the bag.

✦ 61 ✦

AIN'T SHIT SWEET.

M ale'Rose, Tiny Trey Soljah, Chipmunk, and two others – one being the homeboy robbed alongside Male'Rose – all sit at a table inside Croft Alley diner thirty minutes later. Another group of five men, but younger, occupy the next table several feet over, but who are all a part of the entourage tonight. News of the chain being grabbed is being kept quiet so far between the first table and no one else. After the jackers sped off Male'Rose down played the robbery nonchalant as though it never happened. To help not draw suspicion in that regard, Chipmunk and Tiny Trey Soljah both removed their chains off and had them sent away.

However, Male'Rose seethe with rage and the anger in him can be heard when he expresses his revenge. "Fuck that chain. I'm gon' break their spirits for trying me," he vents.

"Don't trip, bro. Before the sun is up you'll have results. The tracer app on my phone is hitting on a location to the tracker inside the medallion. Dummies has to know that shit is high tech these days," announces Kenu. The fifth person at the table. The fourth's name is Baby Snap, and who was robbed alongside Male'Rose.

"I'm jumping out buss'n on this one," snaps Baby Snap.

Male'Rose repeats the same, of his own behalf. He's anxious to get in the field and bust some heads. Even his trigger finger is now jumpy. But then Tiny Trey Soljah becomes the voice of reason.

"I feel you snap. On Trey- foe I do. You too Rose; on Raskals. But listen Male'Rose, you have more at risk right now if shit get ugly. Like, matha fuckas running to them people once bodies get dropped. And then them people running down on you since you're directly involved. So just hear me out; this is not a situation that definitely calls your hand to front line it. It's not even out there on blast about what happened. So spit your pride out about this one. You have a table over there with all young threats 'ready to go' about anything, without question, if any of us say go! Let Baby Snap handle it," Tiny Trey Soljah reasons with patience. "Believe me Crim, I feel your rage. But I would want you to pull my rag the same as I'm pulling yours now; as you've done before."

"Damn. That just woke me back up because I was sitting here at first and thinking the same about J.O.Bing with you, Rose. But the lok is right. And we haven't made it this far, still grooving like we in khakis and chucks. No matter how close in the mud will still stump," voices Chipmunk on second thought after hearing Tiny Trey Soljah out.

The table quiets for a second. Then a thought occurs.

"Stump? That's the phrase the clown that peeled me used. Then he told the clowns with him they out in eight seconds. But, he said 'eight seconds' like if he banged it," recalls Male'Rose.

"Stump? That's too common to pin point to anyone specific. You see I used it. But now if he banged eight seconds, that may narrow shit down to someone," answers Chipmunk.

The table grows quiet again. This time for several long seconds. "Damn. Crim tried us."

"Who!" Snaps Baby Snap at Tiny Trey Soljah who now stares out the diner's window with an evil grin on his face.

"The boy form eight-eight seven. This is what he do as a profession. He book shit all around the industry in L.A.: ball players, rappers, celebrities et cetera. Shit, he stripping bitches and all," begins Tiny Trey Soljah. Still staring out the window and half grinning as he talks.

"He keep a different crew, putting them together as he goes. Basically whoever with it amongst the sets he fuck with. Tonight can't be messy. 'Cuz dude has to learn a lesson!" Tiny Trey Soljah locks eyes with his reflection in the diner's glass window. A small commotion erupts at the next table over, before quickly quieting. Though now three of the young threats stand and huddle over the table looking down at the other two's phones being held out to see. Then one of the two sitting now stands but walks over to the first table with his phone in hand.

"Look! Ya'll seen this? When did this happen?" the youngin then shows his phone to the table.

Male'Rose, Chipmunk, Tiny Trey Soljah and the other two all look down at the phone. A video clip shows several masked men with one of them holding up the Cuban lynk chain with Stanky Banky medallion. They all mouth off a bunch of obscenities. But then one taunts: "Anybody can get it snatched in 'eight seconds'. Including you! Ya'll know what it is."

"Where you find this!" snaps Male'Rose.

"It's on World Star. Got posted like ten minutes ago. This shit fake cap, right?" asks the youngin.

No one answers. Taking the response as que to mean something serious is going on, the youngin cuts off the video clip and returns to his table instructing that the second phone be turned off as well and for the group to chill silent.

"I guess that changes things now," comments Chipmunk amongst his table.

"Not necessarily. But to some degree it does. Still, we have to stay focused lok!" reaffirms Tiny Trey Soljah.

"Well one things fo'sho, something got'ta shake fast. These clowns think shit sweet. Ain't shit sweet!" Snaps Male'Rose.

"I got it!" Announces Kenu excitedly about the address to where the medallion is located. "And trip this; whoever has it is out this way close by."

"Yeah it's him," Tiny Trey Soljah confirms aloud but more to himself.

"He be out this way in North Hollywood so he can stay close to the bag and get there quick in all directions to where those with the bag party, live, and be."

"Oh if he's out this way then I got'ta play ball! He right here," protest Male'Rose.

"Hold up, Rose! Start thinking lok," interjects Chipmunk. "First of all, the dummy chain we each have of our pieces are in the car, right? Well listen, go sit in the car and put yours on. Then snap and post a pic of you wearing it on Instagram. Don't respond to World Star or anything its talking about. Just comment that you're on your way to the studio or something. Tiny, I need you to call and get us a 'Go-Mobil' here, A-sap! Kenu. How far are we from that address?" Ask Chipmunk.

"Like, less than ten minutes," reports Kenu.

Male'Rose stands quickly from the table and immediately leaves the diner out into the parking lot and climbs in one, out of the three, Raiths parked there.

"I know what you're thinking T.S. But look, if we send the young homies it'll only make noise. This calls for our hands so that it goes quiet and smoothly with no loses. Me, you, and Baby Snap can handle the wax. While Kenu and Male'Rose take the young homies and push back to the studio. Something has to be done T.S., either way. So trust me," now reasons Chipmunk. Chipmunk stares at his groove-dog for a response but who seems lost in deep thought about something. Though clearly it is relative to the present dilemma.

Tiny Trey Soljah finally blinks and looks at his entrusted comrade. "I trust you! That's not the issue. I'm with you lok; especially now. So say no more, we're groovin' in silence. Time to play with magic."

Stanky Banky

The night is dark and chill with a bit of wind that starts to pick up. On a quiet street at this hour no one is out except for one person who pushes a baby stroller hurrying along the sidewalk then turning into a triplex of houses lined one after the other in unison. The stroller and its covered up bundle inside bounce around a bit from being driven over cracked and bumpy concrete. Small rocks grind or crunch beneath the pushers footsteps passing the first house and coming up on the next…

Inside the second house along the row, men loft about inside still awake late in to the night. They have just passed on a liqk and are feeling good about the reward. The leader of the bunch cashes out his younger accomplices while at the same time praising them for their participation. He rocks the chain with Stanky Banky medallion around his neck.

"Everybody did their thing and played their part to a 'T'. You all stood up tonight. That's what I need and expect out of young hittas; to play your position. You see how shit went greasy? That's how you strike in 'eight seconds'. And that's how you eat! You feel them ten bands each in your hands? Yeah, that's right. Eat young hittas: Eat! I had to come out my own pockets and feed you now than wait till I cash this bitch out; only because of ya'll performance tonight. Keep it that way."

The leader gas up the young boys while quickly cashing out forty grand. He isn't tripping for the chain alone he can get at least his forty grand back from whoever he dumps it off to or fence it. And if Male'Rose post anything asking for his loss back, or spread word in the streets for it, then it's going to run him one hundred and fifty grand in all stacks. Which he is hoping plays out that way. It is why he boasted about the heist on WorldStar, to secure the full value of his liqk put down. No rapper wants to be known for getting his chain snatched. And surely not for never getting it back. Even if one has to pay for it back. Not to mention the icy bracelet Male'Rose had around his wrist. That's worth another twenty grand.

"A, say, look out the window and see who's that I hear coming this way," now instructs the leader to one of the young hittas. The youngest out the crew, a seventeen-year old proudly looks out the window, feeling geeked about playing any position giving.

"Looks like some square pushing a baby inside a stroller and cold as fuck. He got'uh be going to o'l girl house in the back with all them kids. This probably baby daddy number five," laughs the young hitta and draws laughter from his cronies, as he then watches the person pass by before leaving the window.

Hearing the comment made inside, from the half open screen window, instead of stopping, the stroller pusher pushes on. Its jacket pulled tight and zipped all the way up with the collars flipped. Sporting a dark Santa stock beanie cap with matching knit gloves. He keeps on to the back as expected. Thankful to have patience.

At the last house the stroller stops and the pusher quietly steps onto the porch to knock at the door. But instantly from the bedroom window a few feet over, loud groans from a man followed by low moans from a woman can be heard, even over the Jacquees song playing from inside. Then the woman warns, "hurry up before my man gets home!"

Well damn, the pusher thinks, it would be too late now if he was her man or baby daddy number five. But he's neither and quickly dismisses the thought of humor while reaching down into the stroller to pick up his baby.

Stanky Banky

Male'Rose steps inside the recording sound booth and places the headphones on, then adjusts the mic to his height. Without any pad or paper he is ready to go and let what comes off his chest flow. Being peeled for his jewels has him in his body, coupled with the fact that he isn't out in the field and murking something about it.

However, he knows that his J.O.B loks is going to bang something tonight and make it look sexy, for him having to feel naked around the neck and wrist.

Kenu, who is also the record label's studio engineer, gets behind the sound boards. And one out of the five younger homies from the diner but also looking to get on as producer making beats, plugs in his iPhone then plays a track he knows Male'Rose should feel. And he does. In fact, everyone in the studio listening finds it catchy. The track has that murking sound and feel to it, with a sample from Keith Sweat's "Nobody" record to make it smooth. A perfect combination. Male'Rose closes his eyes and feels it.

"Nobody, Nobody, Nobody but me – is fucking wit' me!" growls Male'Rose over Keith Sweat's vocals.

Kenu presses a button that then loops and double the vocals of Male'Rose over Keith Sweat's and now Keith's vocals sound like an ad-lib. Which now makes for the hook. Seconds after the hook plays from the top, Male'Rose releases his thoughts:

'I then been on top of that stage/ a hunn'it-k on the chain/ dice games and at the clubs too and not a hand ever tried to snatch it loose/ but if it do/ I ain't tripping dude/ you a stick up kid/ I support you too/ when I double back you can keep the chain/ I want your life lok and your kids too/ your whole crew get hit up too/ when the grave full then cop the duce/ but if you call the cops on some hot shit. Bet the cops tell you don't call them/ 'cuz my gunz bark at the cops too/ what? / you thought I'm a nigga too/ I'ma black man/ with a strong hand/ treat a lesbian like a fag too/ send them both too to the fire squad/ I got sons to raise and a daughter too/ my momma weak not her oldest child/ and my father broke not his son too/ when my alum drop I want platinum too/ but if don't fuck it I'ma trap too/ and I ain't talking drugs for the feds to come/ I'm in the corporate league with a Jordan plug/ just do it!'

'Nobody, nobody, nobody but me – fucking with me!'

Stanky Banky

Chipmunk steps away from the stroller with a fully baby chopper in hand equipped with a built in silencer. There is no need for cocking one into the chamber, that's been done. He blows into a ear piece mic to give the signal that it's time to play ball…

Flames with bullets spit into the house through the still half open window. Bodies pop-lock, crumble, or drop while at the same time the front door's locks are being shot off and the front door pushed in.

Tiny Trey Soljah and Baby Snap enters the residence and finishes off who isn't deceased already. They each have baby choppers of their own, equipped with silencers and a shell casing net attached to each weapon's round chamber. The same as with Chipmunk's weapon, who silently goes and recovers the baby stroller, placing his baby back inside then disappearing from sight. Leaving no trace behind. Inside the residence, Tiny Trey Soljah and Baby Snap give their victims whether still breathing or not, all head shots for thinking shit was sweet. Then magic appears.

Tiny Trey Soljah finds the leader sprawled on his back hit a few times yet still breathing and conscious. The two lock eyes and clearly recognize each other. The leader, with the small bit of strength he has left, removes the heavy chain with medallion from around his neck and tosses it over at the feet of Tiny Trey Soljah who picks it up and stuffs it into his jacket's left pocket.

"It has a tracker in it, huh? Yeah I slipped on that. You got me, lil cuz. But you know this is what I do; I fed you before, like them, when you were hungry," reminds the leader. Then suddenly he coughs up a spit of blood.

Tiny Trey Soljah didn't need the reminder, he had already given long thought, before arriving, to the times before he later met his big homey Joe that blessed him truly. But before Joe, it was the leader now laying here that threw him a small bone from a liqk he sent him on.

"Yeah, you right. You peeled off all the meat from the bone and threw me what was left of it. How I'm quite sure you did with this crew tonight. It's cool tho'; I respect what the lesson taught me then. Like again of your actions tonight. You have no cut card."

"Lil cuz, let me make it. You got the chain back and you did your thang in here with knocking my little crew down. It is what it is. I respect it," pleads the leader.

"Don't nobody grimy respect anything. That's why you're in this predicament now. Oh yeah, and the chain," Tiny Trey Soljah reaches into his jacket's right pocket. "You're going to wear it after all. And since you put it on blast, Worldstar will definitely always remember you. Where is your phone!"

Outside, the Go-Mobile pulls up to a stop out front with Chipmunk behind the wheel. His comrades join in before the vehicle then escapes in the night.

❖ ❖ ❖

Stanky Banky

Back at the studio, Male'Rose finishes the track entitled: "Nobody, But Me!" He loads it up to iTunes and all other music media. Within a hour the song does two hundred and thirty thousand units downloaded. As a bonus track he adds the song to his album to be released the following week...

Within the same hour, a new video post on Worldstar featuring the leader still wearing the chain he boasted snatching in the prior video clip posted forty-five minutes before, but now his brains is blew out from a single shot to his forehead. Very gruesome. Still, the post receives over two million views and still counting...

The following week on a episode of TMZ, TMZ reporter Raquel Harper entails the gossip around town:

"Allegedly it was being reported at first that a member of Stanky Banky had their chain snatched based on a video post on WorldStar. But now that has been quickly disregarded or at best is left questionable. There are only three chains with these big Stanky Banky medallions, each costing two hundred grand a piece, made and owned. And each member of the record label that possess one has come out and stated recently they are unaware of any incident occurring where one of their own chains were snatched or even stolen from them. Then each respectively posted a picture of their chains on social media. Now the rapper, Male'Rose, who since has released a album this week in the wake of all this drama and gossip, album has sold platinum reported on soundcloud. So ku-dos to him and Stanky Banky Entertainment who all came out last night to celebrate, and had their chains on, turning up at club V-Live in L.A." the segment then flashes to photo clips of Stanky Banky in the club. "Oh, and 'ouch' to the guy in the video clip posted on WorldStar with the fake chain on. Whatever that was about. But I'm sure that second post had to hurt." TMZ.

THE FULL MOON.

The Jet Blue flight from JFK airport to LAX lands an hour before midnight. Out of the plane's terminal exits Orange'mist pulling along her small satchel suitcase on wheels. Fear and anxiety still grips her inside. But she holds a calm poker face outwardly. For now that is. The last ten hours of her life has been a frightening and baffled mess. So much that her mind has shut out and blocked from her memory most of what had transpired. The only thing that she recalls, or wants to recall, is being with him one minute and them enjoying their evening out together, to next trying to revive him after he passed out unconscious somehow. Then last, grabbing her things in a panic before leaving the large condo. Praying and hoping that all would be well.

Outside of the airport now, Orange'mist hales a taxi. Once into the cab she dials Miss Six's cell number for the fifteenth time and still without answer. 'What the hell. Six, where are you???'

She screams inside her head.

Stanky Banky

Back in Manhattan, Ron is found inside of a high-rise con-do unresponsive by paramedics that arrive on scene after being called by the owner of the place who had come home after out partying for days to discover the horror. The owner and Ron were friends, and he too works as an independent photographer. Though one that is quite financially successful in the profession. He had known Ron for years, and had given him a key to his place long ago to crash whenever in town. Though he hadn't seen Ron in months. However, because of their work and lifestyles, the absence in between visits wasn't unusual. No different than himself not being home in four days. Now on the night that he returns he too finds his friend; dead. And from what appears to be an overdose.

Stanky Banky

The curtain of the motel room's window draws back just a peak, then closes. The T.V. inside the room plays at a low volume as the occupant in the room sits back down in a chair. Then takes a drag from the joint of weed in hand. A second joint, specially rolled, lays atop of the dresser just in case…
"Excuse me, miss, but we're here."
Orange'mist, far off in a daze, comes to and scan the unfa-miliar surrounding of her destination. A good thing she had her eyes closed during the twenty minute ride, making it appear that she was sleeping. Or else the driver would have picked up on the fear and anxiety she is fighting to not consume her.
"Thank you. How much will it be?"
After paying her fare, Orange'mist exits the taxi and rolls her suitcase along into the motel. She doesn't stop nowhere but at the room number she received in her last text from Miss Six six

hours ago and before rushing to catch her flight. She desperately can't wait to meet her, just for the blanket of security if nothing else. The incident with Ron has scared the soul out of her. Now she wish she hadn't gotten herself involved in the whole ordeal to begin with.

But the bitter truth is, she wishes she hadn't flirted with Ron to begin with. Being how she arched her back to poke her ass out, or in how she smiled seductively, both, for the camera during the rapper guy's photo shoot. Putting it on a little extra thick. And thinking she was being cunning about it just for the play of tease with Ron. But Miss Six peeped game. Something only another sneaky freaky bitch would catch. "Damn, Miss Six," she had thought at the time. "Miss something sometimes." Besides, Chipmunk was present during majority of the photo takes and so most of the times her actions were to catch his eye and arousal. Her true intentions. Not Ron's attention.

However, the photographer made a pass at her after the photo shoot was finished. Openly showing interest in her, which she found to be cute and different. The handsomely dark Turkish, with thick but smooth accent, had some game about himself with a lady. And she found that attractive.

But too, Ron had horney perv written all over him. And for certainly Miss Six read all of that even with her eyes closed. Orange'mist knew it. But not until two days ago did Miss Six start to encourage her to go out to New York after Ron called to invite her the week before to come spend the weekend with him…

The door opens after the first knock and Orange'mist hurries inside, now feeling a whole lot better. Miss Six shuts the door close behind her. Orange'mist stands her suitcase against the wall then goes and flops down on the bed, sitting upright.

"How come you haven't answered your phone. I called like fifty times," exaggerate Orange'mist a bit.

"I've been running around doing this and that to make sure things remain in order. I accidentally left my phone at home before I drove out to here," answers Miss Six nonchalantly. She looks Orange'mist over skeptically. Detail meant everything right now.

"So what is this. What are we doing here?" ask Orange'mist, clueless.

"That's what we're about to figure out now," Miss Six's brown eyes turn a dark hazel green as she continues to look Orange'mist over knowingly.

"I use to dream of owning this place, The Full Moon, when I was younger," Miss Six continues. "I turned my first trick when I was seventeen at this motel. In fact, in this exact room. I rode his dick right inside that Jacuzzi there."

Several feet from the single room's front door, a Jacuzzi tub with mirrors around the wall of it is stationed atop of tile flooring. Then there is the single bed several feet over from the Jacuzzi, a closet, a dresser, t.v., and last a bathroom with shower stall.

"I was thinking about running the water and sitting down in it before you got here. Just to chill and smoke a joint. But I fell asleep first and took a nap. I guess I got tired. You just woke me." Miss Six takes her leg and crosses it over the knee of her other beneath the robe she wears. She is seated in the same chair she has occupied the entire time she has been inside the room.

"Anyway, you look like you might ought to sit down inside the Jacuzzi and take a chill pill. You look a step from stepping over the edge. Girl what's wrong?"

But before Orange'mist can answer, over on the t.v. a news flash airs. A photo of Ron is shown, as the reporter reports the photographer's death and the speculation of possible overdose as the cause of death. A second photo is then shown but of the deceased longtime friend and famously known photographer whose high-rise condo the deceased was found in, and by, unresponsive.

"Oh-My-God. Nooo, he died," Orange'mist jumps up from the bed in gray shock, then immediately falls back on the bed now in total fear. Miss Six shows no emotion.

"Girl, who? Calm down. You're shaking," snaps Miss Six. She doesn't bother looking at the television, the report has already aired twice in the past hour. She kept the t.v. on purposely for this reason.

"I can't! That's the guy I was just with in New York, Ron. He's dead now," cries Orange'mist literally with tears. This infuriates Miss Six who shows no sympathy.

"Toni, what happened!" snaps Miss Six. Referring to Orange'mist by her true name.

"I don't remember, really. Last night we went out and kicked it. Then when we got back in he wanted to do some coke but ran out of the stuff he had and so I gave him the coke you had given me before I left out there. To keep him from spending money that could go in our pockets. That's what you told me to do, right? But after that I can't recall what happened…" Orange'mist pauses. Her eyes flutter with nervousness. "But then I recall waking up late this morning and finding him laid out unconscious. I tried to revive him but…I can't recall if it worked… I just remember grabbing my suitcase and leaving. I called you I remember now too because that's how I got the flight information and what I.D. to use for the ticket to get straight back to L.A…. but that's it… that's all I remember… that's why I kept calling you…"

While Orange'mist rambles on in tears or pausing to wipe them, Miss Six has already gotten up and starts to fill the Jacuzzi tub with water. She had heard enough and knew everything already. For starters, the coke Orange'mist gave to Ron was pure raw uncut Perubian. And as planned the junkie snorted a dose too much for his heart to hold. But to ensure his fate, Miss Six was always on the scene the entire time.

However, she wouldn't have had to step in if Orange'mist sneaking, lying ass hadn't sniffed a small bit of the dope off her fingertip first. And before Ron indulged. Now luckily for her that's all she did. Orange'mist had gotten with Ron, or the thought of being away from Miss Six for a while and abandoned the rule of not getting high while on a date, or indulging in any drug other than marijuana for that matter. Indulging in hard drugs was a sure way to fall off of your game or be later tricking just to get high; becoming the trick. Or as happened in this scenario once that small bit of coke got into Orange'mist's system, she forgot about the obstacle and instead became the obstacle of being Ron's nasty amazon slut to run through. Sucking him off for hours and letting him bust all over her face. Then him watching her wipe it with her hands and lick it off of her palms and fingers. To next licking his balls and then eating his ass. And later him cumming in her ass before it was all said and done, and she later passing out asleep. By the time Ron did a line of the kill dope he was up and alone by himself. Drained of cum.

Miss Six waited patiently before coming out of hiding in a hall closet of the condo, after she was lucky to sneak into the unlocked condo an hour after Ron and Orange'mist returned from their night out together. Prior to that, she had too been inside the club they had gone to, and waited outside the café lounge afterwards. Paying attention to detail.

Later when she stepped from out of the closet, she found Orange'mist naked and passed out asleep and Ron sitting hunched forward on the sofa barely shallowly breathing. That's when she hit him herself with a shot of the raw coke left out on the table. Securing the overdose. Then she quickly left the condo, leaving a now awakening Orange'mist behind, to go and set up for what could be possibly next.

"Miss Six, I'm scared. I can't go to jail for this."

Miss Six turns from the Jacuzzi to stare again at Toni. She refused to see her as Orange'mist by which the name originally derives from a dear friend of hers who is now an incarcerated Assata and who she named Toni after. The original never showed fear and was a stump down rida. Miss Six looks at Toni and thinks of what it then came to after a two year run. But Miss Six has gained too much in life to lose it now. And second, but not least, wasn't no lying, sneaky, conniving, weak bitch going to compromise her and jeopardize the wellbeing or freedom of her 'heartbeat'!

"Go to jail for what? You haven't done anything," calmly replied Miss Six. This time swallowing her anger and disgust.

"But news said Ron had overdosed! And I gave him the coke he took; that you gave me to give to him. We're both in trouble now," cries Orange'mist.

"No we're not. Trust me! Haven't I always been right. So listen to me you need to try and relax. We're good sista girl. Come on! Let's get in this Jacuzzi. I'm readying with water. And smoke a 'J'.

Then we can discuss this some more once your mind and nerves settle down. Okay? The water is warm."

Orange'mist undresses to her panties and bra then follows Miss Six into the Jacuzzi still filling with water. She instantly starts to readjust the hot and cold knobs to heat the water. It isn't warm as Miss Six claimed.

As planned, Miss Six excuses herself to go fetch the joint of weed from dresser before returning to the tub and handing Orange'mist the joint with a couple striking match sticks.

Orange'mist lights up with the first strike and takes a much needed long drag from the joint. She holds the smoke in for nearly a minute before exhaling it. She begins to calm while fully seated in the Jacuzzi now. She takes a second pull while Miss Six, without discarding her robe, has a seat stop the Jacuzzi's tile countertop lining the tub of it. Her feet break the still rising water.

By the third pull and before she can think to pass the joint, Orange'mist is stuck. The laced joint of weed, now floating in the water, practically paralyzes her. Her body is stiff and now numb to the water that begins to rise past her chest. Still continuing past her chin.

Miss Six stands out and away from the Jacuzzi, completely ignoring Toni, as she cleans up behind herself. She pulls her clothes out the closet and dresses back in them. Then checks herself in the bathroom mirror to assure that her appearance is the same as when she first checked into the room. She didn't need to watch a UTube video to learn how to commit the perfect murder. The streets had already taught her well.

Before she was known as Miss Six she was called Sixteen. Because when she was sixteen years-young she was raw and ruthless for a girl. But too because of her height and beauty had to remind grown men around the hood her legal age and the risk taken if they still played.

Then she became Miss Six after she started using her sense to have cents; in six figure digits. But even then only after she had first, grown six feet tall; and had six bodies.

Stanky Banky

The water from the Jacuzzi overflows past Orange'mist's later found lifeless body and onto the floor throughout the room. The case by police is being treated as an accidental death, possible suicide, due to the hard severe drugs found in her system confirmed by the later toxicologist report. However, homicide is not being ruled out yet. Few witnesses spoken to by police and detectives each described the same: an unknown tall man in overcoat, with hat, and large dark shades, was last seen leaving the room the deceased girl's body was found. Late into the early morning's night.

DIVINE TRIO

Chipmunk sits at the head of the table, chews and swallows a delicious mouthful of chicken casserole home cooked from his wife. Before forking from his dinner plate another carving taste, he takes a warm look around the dinner table. His son Eric, now eight years of age, is a spit image of him. He chuckles to himself watching his son who looks up to him, father like son, eat like him too — mashing into his plate of food, hungrily. His wife of seven years now, Bonita, and seated at the opposite end of the table, smiles knowingly at the two of them.

Father, son, mother. Or said: 'Father, Son, Holy Spirit'. The Universal Trinity of Man, Woman, and Child. In that order. For Chipmunk this was a life unimagined fifteen years ago. Or a life he ever had his son's age. Though still from him was created this present life he feels humbly blessed to have. Yes, truly humble.

He first met his wife when she was twenty-four years young and he was nineteen. She was solid and down to earth. A sweet square bear he called her. From the royal parts of the state of Indiana. The two first met at a bank in Hammond, where Bonita worked as a manager, back when he and Tiny Trey Soljah use to traffic marijuana to Gary and Indianapolis. He would deposit large sums of cash into his savings, and his financial investment accounts, each, at her bank. She was the first to open the door between them, and ever since then he has been the man of her heart and soul.

A single child from a small suburban family of moderate wealth, Bonita was raised by her wedded parents who are both educated and working class people, now retired. And too, her now eighty-six year-young grandfather who has been in her life since day one. A land owner that still grows vegetables, and breeds live stock now for over fifty years. Bonita had been instilled with principles and morals her entire upbringing. She was family oriented; and she honored her creation as woman in God's great Kingdom, and in her marital relationship without ever stepping outside her role thinking to pose as a man upon a man. Chipmunk had himself a wholesome woman and wife, and that gave herself to him still a virgin. She was smart-sweet-submissive. The three perfect 'S's in a perfect woman. A moral character in principle his big homey Guerilla Joe taught him to look for in a woman as soul mate. If she didn't already have the three 'S's in her, then to teach her to build her. But if she couldn't or wouldn't learn, then be rid of her fast because she will only be drama and pain. Ultimately weakening to a man's mind and soul.

But Bonita was everything but drama or pain, or a weakness. She was spiritual balance and strength to his mind, body, and soul.

"Baby, your phone is beeping." Still smiles Bonita, vibrantly. Chipmunk retrieves his phone from his pants pocket finally. He had wondered off in deep thought, thinking about his wife and son, and didn't hear his cell phone alerting him of a text message. He looks down at the screen of his phone. The sender of the text reads unknown. But the coded message is clear. The three number digit: 1-8-3, meant but one thing; from only one person. His L'Ok Bitch.

Stanky Banky

He hasn't seen her since the night after Male'Rose's photo-shoot with Ron. Almost a month ago. He had made time then to spend the night with her before returning home to L.A., and they shared a presidential suite she had reserved back at the Bellagio before coming into the restaurant where lunch was reserved.

The following night, after he held her in bed after a hot oil bubble bath together, a dinner she cooked and prepared herself, and a good comedy they watched while smoking a 'J'. Still, that night he would not, and did not, penetrate her. She lay in bed, till falling asleep, with a hot wet pussy and just his hands tight between her thighs mounted with the warmth of his body against her skin. Enough to satisfy her; she wasn't completely bothered. This type of behavior from him, and before she took care of an assignment he'd given her, wasn't uncommon. It only built up for the love making to come…

Chipmunk pulls into the Carlton Square in Inglewood, California. The security guard in booth at the secured entrance/exit gate, waves him through welcomingly without question. Five years ago he purchased one of the biggest homes, at $1.3 million, inside this upscale community of middle to upper class Blacks, mostly. However, the purchase at the time was done so mainly as a gift. As promised he would buy this Mission Revival style house for the one he shares the home with. Which isn't a secret from his wife; or his wife a secret from his L'OK Bitch…

Miss Six meets her 'heartbeat' as she stands in a door frame of the house that leads from inside-out into the garage. A Maserati enters and parks alongside her CLS and the garage shed electricity close…

Chipmunk emerges from the Maserati and greets Miss Six with a long awaited passionate kiss. It reminds her of the very first kiss they shared, only now more passionately done: slowly, calculative, and moist than wet. Back then, a decade ago, she had barely turned sixteen but had a crush on him for two years prior. Although only a little over a year older than her, he didn't pay her any mind at first. Not until after she became sixteen, by name than age, did he start to pay her attention.

The occasion came on their first mission together, but her first period. He had jumped out buss'n and chased down a rival, while she stayed behind the wheel asthe driver of their getaway. She showed no fear. And surprisingly afterwards, he showed her affection. They kissed and had sex parked in an alley inside the same car they'd just done dirt in.

Later again the same night, he took her on a second mission. But this time he made her hop out and 'get it' like a bitch off the leash. And she did. And again he kissed and fucked her good all in the same night. She was hooked now and wanted to go on a mission all night, every night. But none of it then or now would have been, had she not first showed that she wasn't just some pretty girl in the hood looking to be the next hoodrat on the block. But instead, a L'OK Bitch!

Dressed in a small silk night gown and nothing else, Miss Six lifts a leg and pins her thigh back against the door frame she's now wedged in between. Chipmunk steps into their kiss while too palming a hand over her heating volcano beneath the gown. He rubs her mountain until the entire landscaping is slippery wet and he can feel the now harden clitoris in between his thumb and forefinger. He twirls it softly then pulls his hand out from under the gown and place two of its wet fingers, in the V-Shape, over her mouth's lips. Then he licks the V-of his two fingers before sticking his tongue through its slit where she meets it with her own; they lock and tongue kiss. And she grinds him back with her pussy over his hard dick bulging inside his jeans. Her fresh cherry-vanilla scent helps to provoke his arousal. Being towered by two inches, Miss Six wraps her arms around Chipmunk's neck who stands at six two for steady balance. This she can never jeopardize for anything or no one; her first and only love.

Though once upon a time, she almost lost all that she and Chipmunk shared and later became. Trying to move fast and thinking she was sneaky. In the beginning he didn't know of her actions with turning tricks for money. Not until around the time she was eighteen and had gotten pregnant. But due to not honestly knowing whether the child would be his or a trick's, she aborted the life. Which later caused her to come clean with him. Because too, that is when she learned in her heart how truly she loved him.

Chipmunk punished her for her behavior. Cutting her completely off. That messed her up psychologically. She rather he had beat her up than to put up a stone wall the way he done. He was the closest thing to her without having much family of her own outside of him but for her grandmother that partially raised her. At times she too was a ward of the state and would runaway form home placements. That was one of the things they shared in common other than the streets being home to them. But she had fucked up. And not until after she cried her heart out for all to see, and chased after him for a year, did he suddenly one day give her an ultimatum. He had feelings for her still. But too, she was his L'OK Bitch; a reflection of him as a L'OK in the streets. That part he would always respect her for. It was the fact that, he couldn't see himself being with a prostitute if that's what she truly was or going to be. Not his L'OK Bitch! But even more so the reason was for him shutting her out was because she had possibly killed his seed. That cut a scar in him mentally that he still punishes her for. Not giving her a child she desperately wants now.

However, and during that time, he himself had just started to get some real money. And now he could afford to put her on or even take care of her. Before then, he couldn't. Which later made him realize that he couldn't completely knock her for doing what she felt could give her the things she wanted or needed. He had taught her the murder game, but not how to hustle. Therefore, he felt that he owed her that much before he then could fully judge her. Or dismiss her. And so he came with an ultimatum.

First, she had to cleanse herself by remaining abstinent from all her previous desires that led up to her actions which caused him to distance himself from her: sex, money, drugs, alcohol, material things, and anything else he later felt could or did pollute her mind. Including bad foods. This she had to do for a full eleven-month cycle. The time it takes for the mind to recondition itself, and the body to rejuvenate anew. Before he would touch her again. Or look her eye to eye. So to assist her he got her an apartment, bought her a bucket car, and took care of her for a year while he monitored her.

Second, and during the eleven months period, she had to read, study, take classes, and learn educative things that later enlightened her about 'self'; in every aspect. But too about the world and the economics of it. Being that money was a necessity in general, then also an attraction of hers. He placed on her many of the same lessons his big homey Guerilla Joe was placing on him at the time, which later made him the wise successful man he became. And is today. And last, he gave her the ultimatum, that if she still chose the profession of running tricks for a bag, then she had better figure out how to do it without ever having to suck or fuck a dick other than his own. Or else he was done with her for good; her choice. It was far too many ways to get the things needed or desired in life than for her to wake up every day sucking or fucking as a hustle or career. And he surely wasn't going to share her pussy with the streets if he truly had her mind.

But indeed he did have her mind. Miss Six wiped her eyes, put on her big girl panties, and woke the fuck up. Especially after Chipmunk went from a '85 Regal to pulling up on her in '98 SC300 Lexus of the same year. After doing so she then began bossing up herself. And later, she only went back to the hoe game, but as a hustler than prostitute, because the game was way too sweet. Using Chipmunk's lecturing and disciplining of her, she did her research, studied, and learned the game from a professional entertainer view. Than her before renegade's frame of thought. And to her discover, she learned that there were different types of tricks and all sorts of pervs. And that those who didn't seek penetration or oral sex were the tricks that paid the most for their weird or freaky fetishes. Later on when she showed Chipmunk a million in cash and told him he can keep it, it was all on a trick, he then seen in her something anew: smart-sexy-submissive. The three 'S's in a Bad Bitch.

But instead of accepting her money he didn't want or need by then, he encouraged her to put her mind to use again, in figuring how to invest the cash into something legit she could then make a fortune from. And that he would support her 3000%. That's when she came up with the hair care products. Her ticket to bossing up another notch…

The two now lay in bed, Miss Six on top. Her favorite position. She naturally likes to feel in control and dominant. Unless when she is being dominated by him. But for now, she rides him hard and good, working her hips, and arching her back correctly, for one last burst. They have been going now for hours already. Nonstop with making love and now fucking. Chipmunk had just finished dog fucking her like a beast. The way she loves it. Now she is reversing the role for the final lap and putting that wet clamp on him just right.

"Errrah," he busts hard but still manages to stay up a full minute after.

"Ooooh, fuckkk," she screams for the final time as hot lava creams from her volcano. Making this her hardest orgasm of the six she's had tonight. She collapses from it and lay half-conscious awake on his chest. Slowly drifting off to sleep.

Chipmunk lay fully awake, listening to the low breathing of his Queen warrior- Nzynga, but thinking to himself how she and his wife both compliment him as an Ausar and King. One being his Auset, and the other Nebathet. One, the passive-passionate side of him and the other the passionate-aggressive part of him. All together they form a trio. A practice directly relative to the religious teachings of Meta Neta and its illustration of Ausar(-God). An ancient Black Egyptian deity. By which he studies and develops the teachings and practices of.

Now, and after the dilemma with the girl Orange'mist, Chipmunk feels satisfied with the arrangement he already has with Miss Six and his wife. Another woman would have been too much. Not a perfect fit of three. He only entertained the thought before because Miss Six had kept the girl around far too long, and too close. But now that was no more. Toni, named after a legend, had failed the field test and Miss Six quickly cleaned that up. It wasn't divinely meant to be.

But what was divine and meant to be, was: He, his L'OK Bitch, and sweet Square Bear. King, Queen-warrior, and wife. A Divine Trio.

THE SIT DOWN

Two years have gone by. And like the sound of Christmas, there is a lot of joy and toys for everyone. The streets of L.A. predominately, but too the county to its east San Diego, and the I.E.; and then to the north: Bakersfield, Fresno, Sacramento, and the Bay Area today was all a utopia in many parts of its urban streets. Compared to what it once certainly was in most parts- a melting pot for violence, drugs, gangbanging, ignorance, poverty and early death. Although not for all, but for many it was the life conceived.

But now since the Stanky Banky movement and its nationwide spread, minds were being woken from the cause of it. Not only just the streets in general, but all over and throughout parts of the world was being effected. There were less sleeping souls and now more inquiring minds. And because so, every day was more, than not, a peaceful joy and celebration.

Back in the trenches of L.A., Tiny Trey Soljah along with other key officials on his side of field, including Chipmunk, were successfully able to sit down with key officials from rival gangs their gang had been beefing with since even before he had been born, or certainly before he jumped off the porch into the streets gangbanging. And now for the past year it has been a complete cease fire. And because of that, the culture in L.A. has truly began to change. The political structure and discipline set by agreement helped to make for amends that were badly needed to be made, extending years to decades in the streets; for business relationships and opportunities to be achieved. And for many it too became a chance for a cleansing from immoral behaviors that once poisoned minds, families, and overall society in general. Now men were being men again; fathers being fathers and strong leaders of their household, family, or community. And women were gladly reaccepting their divine roles as woman, mother, and nourisher. Overall. But most importantly from this entire turn in events, by structure, many of lives were still living that may instead have likely been deceased had the previous destructive cycle continued. And so the joy of it all was that there was still so much more to be enjoyed and gained in life, now that a pattern to overcome was certified in motion.

Stanky Banky

Back inside of the interior designed, upscale furnished, spacious executive office suite, returns Chipmunk and Tiny Trey Soljah. The occasion is again with their O.G., Guerilla Joe. Though this time neither of them requested the meeting. Instead, the man with the keys to unlock multiple doors, and a thumb that presses many buttons, orders the sit down.

Dressed immaculate in a suit, Guerilla Joe casually stands before a wide window of his office, looking out, when his prestigious protégés announce their arrival. The two are also dressed in suits as before. It is the standard of dress these days now for the three whenever they meet up. Because too, todays sit downs between them are always pertaining to some form of business.

The 405 freeway over pass is heavy with traffic at this hour of day. Guerilla Joe stares out at it some while nursing a train of thought, still several seconds after Chipmunk and Tiny Trey Soljah have seated. He turns from the window and excuses his tardiness.

"I was in deep thought there," he apologizes then takes his own seat. "I called this sit down today," Guerilla Joe continues, "to first properly commend you two; personally. But too, guys around here in corporate America are buzzing about a few of your business acquisitions accomplished: of course one is your independent success with the record label. Not many before you have excelled to the level you have without one of the major labels – Sony, Interscope, et cetera being its parent company: Death Row, No Limit, Cash Money; what Top Dog is doing now with TDE. And now Stanky Banky is added to that list. Next, the Fytness Lyfestyle brand which brought the sharks out into the hunt looking to compromise things by market competitiveness. However, you were able to counteract majority of their moves and force a stalemate. But which left you with the upper hand still. Strategic dynamic doing on you two's part. You've gained a lot of corporate respect from that. In fact, many of my associates now admire you both. Business-wise, that is.

"Last, but not least, Crush Groove. A very lucrative establishment you have there. Providing services for about, what now, twenty percent of the market covering the entertainment industry. That there is appalling. But! The method being used can be no longer. Suspicion of muscling, trapping-extortion, thuggery might I add; not my words of course. But, those are the words that have been circumvented around. And if I'm hearing them this far up in the chain of circles, there must be an immediate silence down below!"

Guerilla Joe takes a quick pause to make sure that his only warning given is soundly understood and being taken heed to. His eyes give way to severe consequences if his warning is not understood. "You two have come a long way, myself included – in that regard. So much that there is no turning back or looking anywhere else but forward. Therefore, certain actions or ways of thinking need not be carried on in the now present, so to not prevent the present from being an entirely new experience.

"We come into this world not only to have, but to also enjoy experiences as spiritual beings. So don't forefeit experiences left to be had by actions that can truncate your freedom or life. To be better successful at this, your method of thought must further mature. Because thoughts are fuel, the energy to all actions and experiences manifested and whatever the condition of the mind is, will be the condition from the quality of thoughts you think. That's the school of thought. This you know already. I'm only being a reminder to you. And so since I'm at it, let me sum it up here and truly get to why I called this sit down, also. It's as important as any reminder I have given today." Guerilla Joe then turns more serious than his protégés have ever seen him.

"Stop leaving bodies behind! In fact, leave the murder game out of thought. Out of thought, out of mind. You're both super up now. Let the transition you have made completely conform you to who you are today: young, successful, intelligent, Black men in 'America'; I say that with emphasis. And so let me stop to make a point than the point I'm getting to but still as important.

"I acknowledge what you two have contributed to the streets abroad and within the set, our Kingdom of Hoova. But now you have to reposition your place in all that. I encourage this now than later. Continue to do what you can, but do it at no risk to your current position in life. Remember that you are up now! You cannot sacrifice that! Because keep this in mind; that if things out there are to go back to retarded, Allah forbids it do, then you've done all you can. What is meant to be will be. You can help influence others to think and do great, but you can only change yourself. You can give them the tools, but you can only make yourself use them. So keep this is mind as well; you have never ever seen or heard of President Barak Obama out in the city of anywhere J.O.Bing, in fighting street gang or drug wards to bring about change at that level. His thoughts of change and peace are required at a higher realm, and for global power and wealth. The same as with my own thoughts today. And now your own, I heavily influence. Start thinking the same difference; comrades!"

Again, the look of the eyes to instill the exact message that needs to come across is also adhered to. But too the severe consequences if not.

"Now back to my initial point I was making for calling this sit down. An intel of mine's came across three cases that all had your signature on it. But of course only I could read it.

"A photo of a dead man posted on social media, wearing a dummy chain duplicate of a chain made in representation of your record label, but reportedly snatched from someone associated with the label. I seen photographs of the work put down. J.O.B. all over it. However, it's now a cold case. Next, a photographer that once worked for you on multiple projects, was found dead from an overdose. But that's not the link in signature here. By itself. But couple the third case with it, things get a little clear. A second overdose: a model slash back page, OnlyFans entertainer slash escort, or what not, found dead inside of a motel room off of Figueroa in the hood. The same girl, prior to her death, featured on a album cover with one of your artist. And the work done by this same now dead photographer. But that's not the icing, Peep.

"The icing is, this dead photographer, prior to, did a photo lay out shoot for the pop star diva who's later exact same home the shoot happened in, was robbed. And lo and behold, the same company being rumored to be involved in thuggery, recovered some of what was taken and that held sentimental value, then returned it. But, under contract of service, of course. Now the cake for this icing; traces of coke found in the model matches the same quality in pure uncut coke found in the photographer's body. One ruled a OD in Manhattan. The other accidental death in L.A.," Guerilla Joe leans back into his chair and has a quick seconds small chuckle to himself. A chuckle that meant he is aware of what's going on.

"No finger prints to worry about in anything I've mentioned. But you do see the connections? Tighten up!" Pausing, he glances up at the mahogany wood on the wall. The time reads, almost noon. "No charges will ever come from any of this, the hand has already been washed on that. Besides, I'm the matha fucking major of L.A. now," Guerilla Joe sits up forward in his chair, cracks the knuckles of his hands clasp together, before laying them still clasp upon his desk.

"However," he continues, "if these same circumstantial connections are ever made then used by an opponent in business, it can make bad for publicity. And bad publicity is bad for business on Wall Street. Which is the only street you two now should be jumping out banging on: for Power and Wealth! Understood!"

Chipmunk and Tiny Trey Soljah both sit backs straight in their chairs. A conscious bomb had just been dropped on them. It was time to awaken to a whole new awareness. This meant even more discipline than ever before and greater dedication to the art form of their work and legacy. The big homey was correct on everything he just pulled their coattails about. And they each felt humble to have him as a real big homey.

True, they had come too far to not go even farther. And, with their own destiny in the each of their palms. Therefore, it was on! And both had the same in mind; that the next chapters of their lives were still going to be Stanky Banky. But this time, all the way banky!

In response to the sit down, Tiny Trey Soljah and Chipmunk reply in chorus. "Overstood!"

Stanky Banky. By Tre Prince ~ THA L'OK

Coming next...Stanky Banky 2

Also read...Bounce Back Joe

ABOUT THE AUTHOR

Tre prince is a native of Los Angeles, California. Born Antoine Lamont Johnson, Tre Prince – also known as O.K. – grew up during the crack era of the 80s, the rebuilding of the 90s, and through the milestones of gangbanging and Black on Black violence in America. Now matured, Tre Prince writes stories that are engaging, exciting, and memorable. Seeing that the mind is key to the outcome of a life lived, he preaches to the streets through characters of fiction in an attempt to give back and help restore a better society for the youth. May his attempts not be in vain… structure to the people!